VANISHED!

A VALUABLE AFRICAN STATUE STOLEN IN SOUTHWEST FRANCE

ROBERTA SAMUELS

Red Penguin
BOOKS

Vanished! A Valuable African Statue Stolen in Southwest France

Copyright © 2023 by Roberta Samuels

Published by Red Penguin Books

Bellerose Village, New York

ISBN

Print 978-1-63777-512-7 / 978-1-63777-514-1

Digital 978-1-63777-513-4

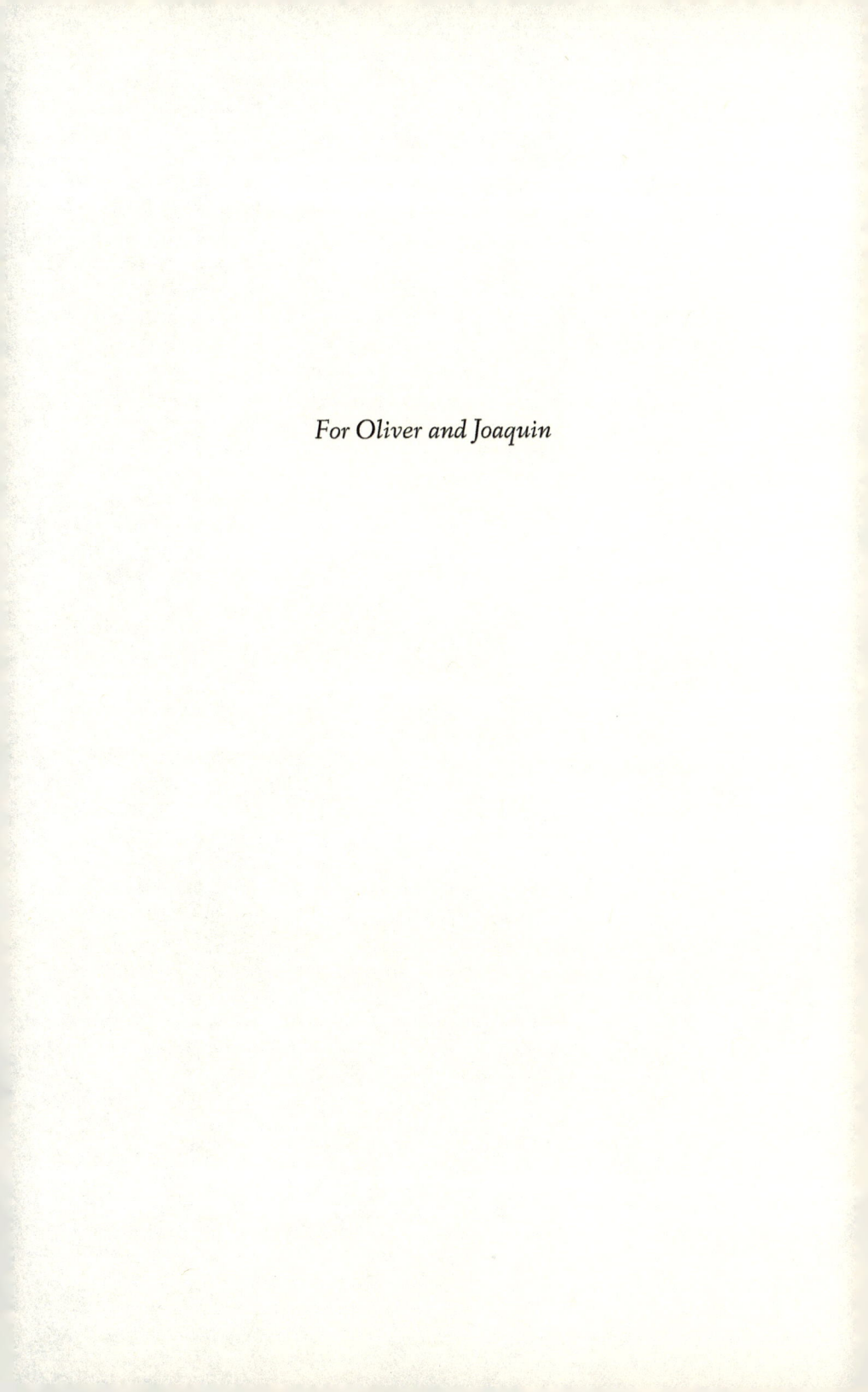

For Oliver and Joaquin

CONTENTS

Note to Reader   vii
Statue   ix
Map   xi

1. An Attempted Kidnapping   1
2. A Tale of Two Brothers in Senegal   7
3. A Visit to le Commissariat   12
4. Abdoulaye and Al Qaeda   19
5. Marianne, the Librarian   26
6. The Africajarc Festival   31
7. Agadez, Niger   37
8. Lunch with the African Art Seller   44
9. The Map, Key to an African Oil Strike   51
10. Destination Morocco   58
11. Abdoulaye's Odyssey Continues   64
12. An Excursion to Normandy   70
13. The Dior Museum   79
14. Chasing the Paraglider   87
15. Man Down   92
16. Florida Bound   99
17. Asking the N'Kisi Kongo Figure for Answers   105
18. All's Well That Ends Well?   114
    Epilogue   120

Book Club Notes   123
Acknowledgments   125
About the Author   127

NOTE TO READER

When I set out to write a cozy mystery about an African carving gone missing in the bucolic southwest of France, little did I think how far astray it would take me.

I would like the reader to know that information in the book that might seem fanciful or exaggerated is based on fact. More information about these subjects is available online.

Not only did I learn a great deal about African 'power figure' statues, but my story also led me to the plight of the Ogoni people who live in the Niger River delta in the south of Nigeria.

The brutal suppression of Nigerian writer and activist Ken Saro Wiwa and the Movement for the Survival of the Ogoni People (MOSOP) described in this book really happened. The Ogoni and the other peoples of River State in Nigeria still suffer the ill effects of pollution from oil exploration. You can find more information about their present struggles on YouTube.

As I crafted the story of Abdoulaye, a fictional Senegalese fleeing his country for a better life in Europe, who had to pass through the troubled area of sub-Saharan West Africa, the plight of migrants and this region was top of the news. The dangers Abdoulaye faces in the book to get from Senegal to Algeria are based on actual problems and occurrences in the beleaguered area of Mali and Niger that he travels through on his journey.

Similarly, the Katibat Macina branch of Al Qaeda does exist, as does its support by the Russian Wagner Group. Illegal migration from Niger toward Algeria and the berm erected to keep migrants from entering there are also real. Melilla, Spain, is an actual place, and the horrific incident at the wall described in the pages ahead really happened there.

Attempting to create a fictional migrant's struggle to get from Africa to France, I gained a deeper understanding of the almost insurmountable odds such a journey entails and the desperation that motivates such an undertaking.

The fascinating beliefs and practices surrounding N'Kisi Kongo statuettes are based on my research, not my imagination.

To appreciate the powerful aura of these 'objets d'art' in person, I recommend a visit to the Museum of Metropolitan Art in New York or the British Museum in London, among many other museums. There are also many excellent art books whose photographs and text are worth a look to better appreciate the stunning beauty and diversity of African tribal artwork, which I feel is underappreciated.

Upon completing this book, I hope the readers find themselves better informed about such matters as I have become, and I hope they will excuse any inaccuracies due to the complexity of the subject matter or artistic license. But most of all, I hope the story is an enjoyable and interesting read.

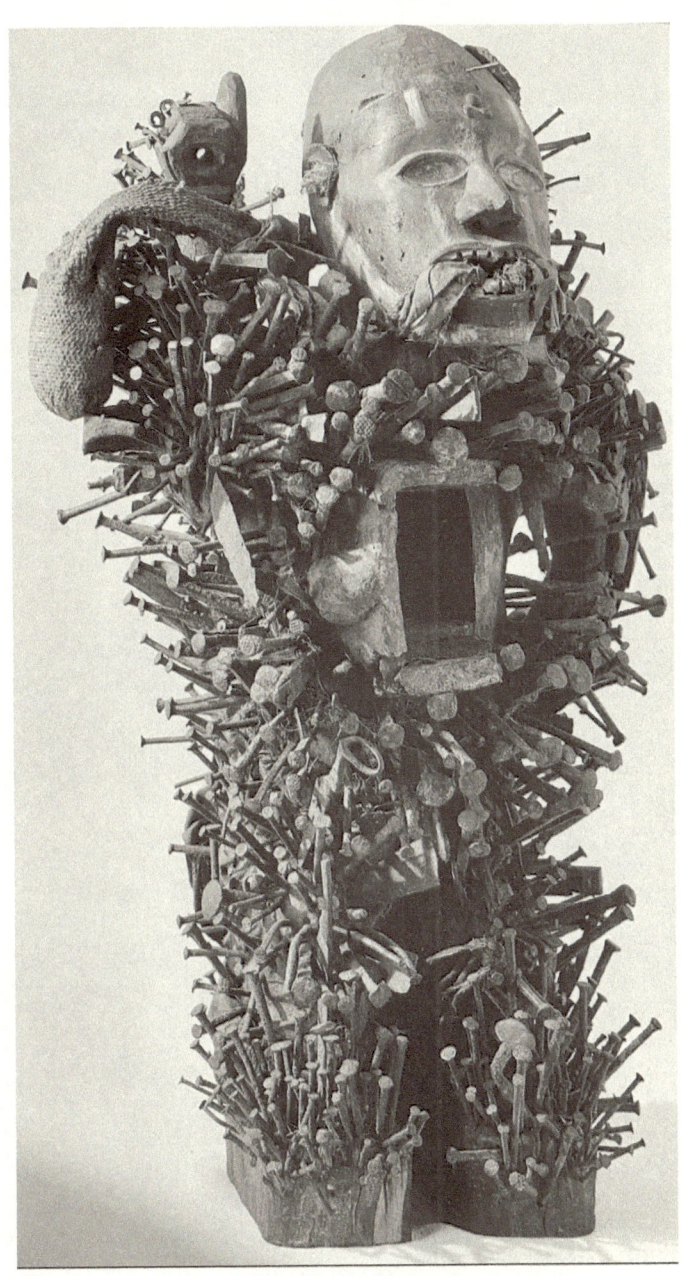

An example of a N'Kisi Kongo 'power figure'

Abdoulaye's Journey

CHAPTER ONE

AN ATTEMPTED KIDNAPPING

T he beautiful young woman's face was wreathed in smiles. Tonight, her long dark hair was piled high onto the top of her head in an elaborate braided coiffure, more high fashion than ethnic. Her mahogany-colored skin glowed against the tangerine color of her blouse, casually left open to reveal a flower-patterned bustier that showed off the tops of her pretty breasts. In her black silk parachute pants and strappy black sandals, she looked sexy and the girl next door at the same time.

The woman's name was Alice, and she warmly welcomed us as usual to the restaurant named for her, *La Table d'Alice*, which she owned with her husband, Édouard. Édouard was a Frenchman with a fashionable, unshaven look. He was several years older than his wife. We speculated to ourselves where he might have found such a beauty as Alice and how he might have made her his own. *In Sénégal, perhaps? In Paris?*

Was the name of the restaurant a nod to the movie and the Arlo Guthrie song? We weren't sure, but as the song suggests, Alice's Restaurant had everything you could ever want, especially if you wanted specialties from our region of France made with the finest local ingredients.

Queenly Alice showed us to our table under the leafy vines shading the patio by the pool and imbuing the dining area with a cooling fragrance that was very welcome on this hot summer evening in Caussade, a bustling and prosperous little market town in the southwest of France an hour north of Toulouse. Although we were sitting just feet from the street, we felt cocooned in our leafy bower.

The heat of the day was abating, but it was still quite light outside. In the summertime, the sun didn't set until around 10 p.m. in our French latitude. I could clearly see my boyfriend, Sam, sitting across the table from me. For a moment, I studied his handsome, slightly off-kilter features, the hair at his temples graying in a distinguished way. At least as I saw it. He was my boon companion, lover, partner in crime, and confidante. He was the light of my life.

Alice's manner was friendly yet professional, as she made sure we were comfortably seated. She and Édouard had transformed the old *Auberge du Chapeau,* formerly a slightly out-of-date eatery decorated with the straw boater hats for which the town of Caussade was known since the 1880s, into a sophisticated but casual restaurant serving excellent renditions of local duck and pork favorites as well as more ambitious seasonal specialties.

"Voici la carte," Alice said as she proffered us the little leatherette booklet that contained the menu. We basked in her warm smile as she inquired about our drink order. *"Je vous sers un apéritif ce soir?"*

"How is Manu?" I asked Alice. She and her husband were the doting parents of an adorable little *métis* boy, Emmanuel, Manu for short. He was a very handsome tot who had inherited his mother's dusky high cheekbones and his father's deep-set blue eyes. At this moment, he was playing on the periphery of the patio dining area as he sometimes did before his babysitter put him to bed. I noticed that there was no *nounou* tonight, and Alice herself was keeping a weather eye on him.

Sam and I were considering whether to have our usual *kir Suze* for drinks before dinner. We were frequent customers of *La Table d'Alice* restaurant. We liked the cuisine and the ambiance. In summer, meals were always served on the outdoor patio, and in cooler weather, diners were seated at tables in the dining room inside the building proper behind the handsome bar. The establishment was an easy 20-minute drive from our French summer house in the village of Montpezat de Quercy.

All of a sudden, Alice's body stiffened, and she let out an anguished scream. Our mouths dropped open, and our eyes widened. A dark-skinned figure in jeans and a tee shirt had grabbed the little boy off of his three-wheeler and was running hell for leather toward the gate at the street entrance. *Where had he sprung from? The kitchen? The corner table?*

Manu set up an anguished, high-pitched wail, "*Maman, Maman.*" It tore at my heartstrings.

Alice shouted in stentorian tones for her husband, who was at his post near the computer screen behind the bar just inside the doors into the restaurant proper from the patio.

"*Édouard, AY DOU AR, viens vite! Aide-moi!*"

"*Édouard!* Help! Come quick! He's got Manu. *O, mon fils!*" she shrieked in a frenzy, taking off at a run after them in her high-heeled sandals. "*Non, non! Arrête!*" she yelled. "Stop! Let go of my son! *Lâchez-le!*"

She ran toward the gate after her baby. The plastic toy he had just been happily riding lay on its side with its big bubble wheels spinning in the air. Sam and I were riveted in place by the unexpected drama suddenly unfolding before our eyes. It all happened so fast. We were paralyzed.

Not Édouard, the boy's father, however. In a flash, his long legs covered the distance from the bar to the gate. Together with his wife, he struggled to wrest their son out of the clutches of the dark-haired man who held the little boy tightly in his arms.

A group of freshly arrived diners was just coming in the gate. Their arrival forced the abductor to slow his momentum a moment to avoid them. This gave Alice and Édouard some catch-up time. As Édouard pummeled the child abductor's head and shoulders with blows from behind, Alice prised the baby away from his grasp in the front.

The assailant panicked and broke away from Édouard's drubbing. He tore off down the street toward the train station parking lot. An incoming diner ran after the kidnapper's retreating figure. He almost caught up to him, getting a hold of the tail of his tee shirt, until it was ripped out of his hand, and the attacker got clean away.

Released from his assailant's vice-like hold, the toddler leapt into the safety of his mother's arms. He was crying pitifully and kept repeating, *"Maman, Papa, Maman, Papa."* His mother whispered comforting sounds into his ear, nuzzling him as she rocked him gently back and forth against her. Édouard stood sheltering his wife and son together in an all-encompassing embrace.

Sobbing and shaking, the little family group clung to one another as I dialed the emergency services, 112, on my cell phone. Sam had a better idea. He stood up from his seat and ran to the nearby police station, which was located just up the street on the main square roundabout near *la Mairie*, Caussade city hall.

"Du calme, du calme, messieurs-dames," said the *gendarme* when he arrived on the scene a few minutes later with Sam right behind him.

"Allons, allons. Qu'est-ce qui s'est passé ici? Now, now. What's been going on here? Ladies and gentlemen, please sit back down at your tables. We will be taking your statements one by one to establish what happened."

He addressed Alice. "Madame Alice, it's alright now," he said kindly, trying to diffuse the situation. "You are *en sécurité.*"

"My family and I will be upstairs above the dining room in our personal apartments," Édouard told the police officer. "We need to settle the baby down. I need to comfort my wife. Call us when you are ready to interview us."

Alice already seemed more composed. Her natural dignity had quickly reasserted itself. *"Merci, Hervé,"* she said to the young man in uniform. All the residents of Caussade knew the town policemen by name. "Just give us a little time, and we'll be happy to tell you what we can."

"Officer," I piped up. "If I may say so, the assailant ran off toward *la gare.* Someone should search for him at the station or on the platform. It might not be too late to find him."

"Très bien, Madame. Our men are already searching the general area as we speak."

Table by table, we were called into the indoor dining area of the restaurant to be debriefed by the head *gendarme.* When Sam and my turn came, we tried our best to reconstruct the attempted baby-snatching from the vantage point of our table. We could recall quite a few details of the kidnapper's dress and appearance, although Sam and I disagreed about just how tall he was.

The policeman took down our statement, we signed and were released. As we were leaving, I thought to myself how pleasant the decor of the dining room was now that Alice and Édouard were in charge of the restaurant. Whereas before, the space had been decorated with old-fashioned Singer sewing machines and examples of straw hats in various stages of completion, the room now featured a rotating display of paintings by local artists. The present artist's paintings were very modern, abstract compositions with bold lines and vivid splashes of color. I found them very appealing. Interspersed among the paintings were a dozen pedestals supporting traditional African sculptures whose dark, angular, humanoid forms stood out dramatically against the honey-colored walls behind them. *Were the sculptures from Alice's personal collection?* I wondered.

As we were going out the door to the patio heading for the street, I turned to ask Sam a question:

"Sam, do you see that wooden figure with the nails in its stomach? Doesn't it remind you of the one we saw at a house sale in Saint-Antonin-Noble-Val a few years ago?"

"My dearest darling, I don't remember. You know, right now, I am focusing on my own stomach, which is quite empty. Let's see if we can find some dinner before the restaurants all close up for the evening. You know how it is around here. Dining hours are strictly regulated in rural France. After 9:30 p.m., no restaurant wants to accept more customers."

"Ooh, you're right, Sam. I'm hungry, too. Let's hurry and see if we can still get into *Les Papilles,* The Taste Buds, on the main square." We rushed off to find some dinner, hoping to put the unsettling episode we had just witnessed out of our minds for a while. *Could this have really happened? And here, out of the way, in uneventful, little Caussade?*

CHAPTER TWO

A TALE OF TWO BROTHERS
IN SENEGAL

Twenty-something years old Senghor and Abdoulaye Diop lived in Saint Louis, a town in Senegal. The Diop family business had always been fishing. The brothers grew up swimming and playing among the sun-dried fishing nets on Saint Louis beach. The native fishing boats were called *pirogues* and were colorfully painted, canoe-shaped vessels that were very maneuverable and sea-worthy. The *pirogues* made a picturesque scene pulled up on the sand, lying hull side up in the sun as the gentle wavelets of the aquamarine ocean lapped at the golden beach.

The Diops were a big, extended family of six brothers and sisters. Abdoulaye and Senghor's older stepsisters from their father's first marriage no longer lived at home. One of them, Alice, was married to a Frenchman she had met at the University of Lagos in Nigeria, where she had won a scholarship. She had grown up in the good years when the family was more prosperous. Alice now lived in France. She had left Africa when the brothers were babies, and they really didn't know her at all.

Life had turned upside down for Senghor and Abdoulaye. Their generation faced entirely new challenges. A double whammy cast a pall over their futures. Rising sea levels forced the family to abandon their house at the beach, which was collapsing into the ocean. The Diops moved inland, away from the cooling sea breezes, to a compound of prefab huts set up by foreign aid agencies. "At least we are safe from being swept out to sea in the next big storm," their grandmother said. And the camp of identical, tent-like houses built on concrete slabs had, with time, become a community.

But there was no employment for the brothers in Saint Louis or in slightly larger Kayar, the next town south on the coast toward Dakar, Senegal's capital city. The Diop's livelihood was fishing, and fishing provided a more and more tenuous income. The catch had dwindled drastically. No sardines had been seen off the coast of Saint Louis for ten years. A *pirogue* that fished out at sea for sardinella stock might have been lucky to catch 300 tons of fish in a year using large seine nets. A trawler that dragged an enormous net behind was able to catch that same amount in a couple of trips.

The fishing nets cast out by hand from the *pirogues* could not compete with the catch snared in the giant nets of the industrial Chinese and Spanish trawlers, which illegally plied the Senegalese coastline day and night. At night, there were fewer patrols around to keep them away, and the trawlers lit up the waters. Senegalese fishermen called it New York City at night. The trawlers' enormous catches obliterated the sea life and their giant nets often degraded the seabed itself.

Abdoulaye told his brother, "I don't think we should risk trying to get to Europe by sea. It's too risky. Let's try going overland. If we can make it to Melilla on the coast of Morocco, we might have a chance to get around the barrier walls there."

Senghor replied. He was the younger brother by two years. "I am with you, and I will follow you, but you know that we might wait years in Morocco for an opportunity to get over the fence into Melilla and Europe. How will we live?"

Even when they successfully arrived in Europe, migrants from Senegal went many years without seeing their loved ones back home while working to become legal residents of Spain. The lucky few sent back money to their families in Senegal. These remittances from Europe paid for the tall, new houses that dotted the skyline in Kayar. Senghor and Abdoulaye dreamt of being one of these successful migrants who could send money home.

Should a migrant worker succeed in proving a steady employment record for at least three years, he (or she, because some women made the trip) could gain legal status in Spain. Spain was one of the few countries where one had the possibility of earning residency in this way. Those who managed to obtain Spanish papers could travel back and forth between Spain and Senegal at will.

But these were the success stories. There was even one former migrant from Saint Louis who was now a member of the Spanish parliament. He was famous in Madrid, and his fellow Senegalese immigrants there applied to him for help with delinquent house payments or other financial emergencies. Almost everyone in Kayar and Saint Louis who talked about this famous man, Serigne M'Baye, used the same phrase. He had a 'fighting spirit.' In Wolof, it was *gnafe kat leu*. You need a lot of fighting spirit to overcome obstacles against all the odds.

Most young men in Saint Louis and Kayar had made several tries to reach Spain but had failed and been turned back —or died at sea in the attempt. Now, it was Senghor and Abdoulaye's turn to try their luck.

The brothers were sitting on the sand, shaded by an overturned *pirogue*, gazing out at the ocean, which was gray and unfriendly looking today.

Abdoulaye Diop shook his head. The brothers had discussed this problem together many times before.

"We can't get ahead of ourselves, Senghor. We can't get discouraged. We'll work it out. We'll have each other. We'll put one foot in front of the other each day for as long as it takes. *Gnafe kat leu.*"

They hugged. The patterns of their plaid cotton shirts blended together as their muscular arms encircled each other's shoulders.

"When do we leave?" Senghor asked. "Let's not put it off any longer. I feel lucky, and I don't want *grand-mère* to suspect we are going. She would be too worried."

Abdoulaye said, "I'm still thinking that we should try a roundabout route to Melilla. If we detour through Mali to Niger, we can stop off for a while with our cousin, Mohamed, who lives in Agadez. We have connections there, and we know that we will have food and shelter for a time. Then rested and refreshed, we can continue north to Morocco and Melilla through Algeria."

Senghor complained, "But that could add months or years to our journey! And we still may not make it into Spain at the very end."

Melilla, Spain, was an anomaly. It was a tiny outpost of Europe on the continent of Africa. A former Spanish colony surrounded on three sides by Morocco and on the fourth side by the Mediterranean. Melilla was administratively part of Spain. A person who made it across the border from Morocco into Melilla was in Spain. And a short ferry ride away from the Spanish mainland and the rest of Europe.

This outpost of Spain was protected by a series of four walls and fences designed to make illegal entry impossible.

Yet some African migrants had made it inside. Fences might be breached or climbed. Sometimes, when political relations were tense between Spain and Morocco, the Moroccan border authorities were inclined to let migrants through. Sometimes, desperation and ingenuity found a way. *Gnafe kat leu.*

CHAPTER THREE

A VISIT TO LE COMMISSARIAT

Back in Montpezat de Quercy, early in the morning the day after the attempted child abduction, Sam bought a copy of the local newspaper, *la Dépêche,* along with his morning croissant and a *pain au raisin* for me. I did love that raisin sweet roll, which was an example of what they called a *viennoiserie* in French.

The bakery was very convenient since it was just down the block from our house. The newsstand was just across from the bakery, so many people made one stop to buy breakfast and a newspaper at the same time.

The owner of the newsstand in Montpezat de Quercy, *le marchand de journaux,* was a *marchande,* Madame Longueville. She was an older woman, a widow, whose daughter helped her run the store where all Montpezat's fifteen hundred inhabitants came to buy their newspapers and magazines.

Before his death, Madame Longueville's husband had been the town postman delivering the news. It, therefore, felt natural that his wife would segue into purveying *La Dépêche* and various periodicals to the residents of Montpezat, *les Montpezatais.*

Before old age made it harder for Madame Longueville to get around, she used to hand deliver a copy of *La Dépêche* to the mayor's house very early in the morning so he could have the news before anyone else. It was a special perquisite she once provided for *Monsieur le maire.* This was long before the days of the internet, of course.

Sam and I read the newspaper aloud to one another as we sat at the breakfast table on the terrace of our new house. We had moved from our 15th-century townhouse a bit farther down the street to a 'new' 15th-century townhouse near the old convent of the Ursuline nuns, which was now part of the Montpezat elementary school. Our new place was in better condition than our former house, which had had some structural problems and leaks. Just like our old place, the new house had an absolutely stupendous view out over the whole valley of the little *Lembous* River as far as the snowy peaks of the Pyrénées mountains on a clear day. We could see the *collégiale* bell tower over the picturesque red tile roofs of the village and all the way to the Provençal-style ironwork cage, which capped the clock at the *Mairie.*

The kitchen, terrace, dining, and living room were together on the top floor of our new house. The bedrooms were below. The ground floor was given over to a guest apartment and a formal entry hall. Since medieval houses tended to be dark and enclosed on the ground floor, where the shop or commercial space had been in the Middle Ages, it was a good idea to put the living space on the top floors in a kind of reverse order. But how to climb up there carrying groceries or whatever on a daily basis? There were always many sets of stairs in a typical house from Montpezat's heyday, *le 15e siècle,* the fifteenth century.

The solution in our new house was an elevator! A prior owner had installed a simple lift, a utilitarian elevator that was cleverly disguised as a set of closet doors on each of *les trois étages*, the three floors. What sybaritic luxury! And also a bit of a necessity as Sam and I weren't getting any younger.

It was sunny up on the terrace at the breakfast table. We adjusted the parasol against the morning sun. Sam read aloud the newspaper's *compte rendu*, summarizing Manu's attempted abduction from his parents' restaurant yesterday evening. The police were asking anyone with information relevant to the event to please come forward.

"I guess that means they haven't found the attempted kidnapper," I said. "What an awful occurrence! Alice and her little family must be traumatized."

"Yes. It says here that *La Table d'Alice* will be closed this week. Sam let out a low whistle. He showed me a photo of an African statuette studded with nails. Listen to this, Barbara."

Monsieur et Madame Édouard Blancpain also reported the mysterious disappearance of a valuable African statue from the dining room of their establishment, where it was on display up until yesterday. The statue is the property of a third party who had lent it to be displayed at La Table d'Alice restaurant for the period of the exhibition. When contacted, the owner was unavailable for comment. The police cannot say if the attempted abduction and the theft are linked. Once again, anyone with information is asked to come forward.

"No way! We saw that statue on our way out of the dining room after the police interviewed us."

"It was there around 9 p.m. We can corroborate that. We should tell the police department what we saw."

"Do we call the Police Nationale, *les gendarmes,* or the

Municipal Police, I wonder? Oh, they've printed the number to call here in the paper. Good."

There were several police forces in France. The *gendarmes* policed rural areas, while the National Police force's jurisdiction was larger cities and towns. They also handled criminal investigations as well as traffic. Author Georges Simenon's fictional *Inspecteur Maigret* was on the National Police, which used to be called *la Sûreté*.

When we called the police, they asked us to come into their offices in a special building near the movie theater in Caussade behind a metal gate. I told them how I had noticed the statue with the nails in its stomach because I had once seen a similar one at a house sale in St-Antonin-Noble-Val a few years ago.

"I was very attracted by its powerful presence. It really spoke to me. I had seen those sorts of objects in the Rockefeller Collection at the Museum of Metropolitan Art in New York. They have an extensive collection of African tribal art in part because Michael Rockefeller, son of Governor Nelson Rockefeller, was an explorer-collector. In fact, he lost his life somewhere exotic. New Guinea, I think, not Africa. The circumstances of his death are unknown. He just disappeared. The Rockefeller family searched and searched for him, but his body was never found."

"Yes, *intéressant*," said the police detective, "but let's get to the point, please, Madame."

Sam took over. "Well, we left the restaurant right around 9:15 p.m., 21h15. I know because I looked at my watch, checking if we had time to find another *resto* for dinner. We both saw the statuette as we walked out of the dining room. Barbara called my attention to it."

"Hmmm," said the policeman thoughtfully. "You definitely

saw nails in the stomach of the African object, n'est-ce pas? Both of you, right?"

We shook our heads in assent.

"Thank you for coming in," the gendarme said.

He didn't seem totally satisfied with our account. Something was troubling him.

"Is there a problem, officer?" I asked.

He looked at us askance. "Thank you for your time. Your information is not entirely helpful. You see, the missing sculpture, the valuable one, has no nails in the stomach area. The one you saw was a different one. A more modern rendition."

"What! *Quoi! Ce n'est pas possible!* There was more than one African statuette with nails on display? Are you sure?" Sam asked the gendarme.

"Madame Alice is certain of her facts. She explained to us that the authentic statuette had no nails in its abdomen. The statue was created and used for ritual purposes by the tribal village in Africa where it was made. The stomach area is where the magical properties of the object reside. The stomach, face, and genitals of these pieces were always left free of nails. You were looking at the newer, less authentic statue."

We chewed over this news.

The police officer continued, "but neither Monsieur nor Madame Blancpain can be sure of the last time they saw the authentic statue with no stomach nails. This makes our job harder. Thank you for coming in, but your testimony doesn't really narrow down the time frame of the theft for us in the way we might have hoped."

Sam and I left the police station and went to find our Citroën *break,* which meant station wagon, under the trees of the parking lot near the movies. It was a *cinéma d'art et essai,* so it showed lots of foreign films, including American movies, along with film festival award winners and children's movies too. You could become a member and get a slightly reduced admission, five euros instead of seven. Admission prices were also reduced twice a year during *les Festivals de Cinéma*.

The trees in the parking lot were those little squat plane trees with the peeling bark whose growth had been arrested by pruning. Their branches were pollarded, radically trimmed, so they grew out instead of up. Without their leaves, they were ugly yet beautiful sculptural shapes. When they leafed out, their big leaves provided good shade, which was welcome in the hot summers.

Sam got into the driver's seat, and I buckled myself into the passenger side. I said, "You know that figure with the nails from the sale in Saint Antonin? I remember the tag said it was called a 'power figure.' I even thought about buying it, but it had such a powerful presence, if you know what I mean, that I wasn't sure if I wanted to display it in our house. I guess I thought it might kind of take over. It had such a strong aura about it."

"What was the price?" Sam asked. "Do you remember?"

"I don't remember exactly, but it was above my budget. That was another reason I didn't buy it. And then, how would I know what something like that was worth? I had no idea."

Sam said, "Let's stop at the *médiathèque* and see if we can find some pictures of these power figures. I wonder what part of Africa they're from. Do you know, Barbara?"

"Quite honestly, no, I don't. I once studied a little bit about Dogon doors, though. I think the Dogon people live in Mali. Their sculptures are very beautiful, and they are especially known for their carved doors. In fact, a lot of the doors feature women's breasts."

"I like that motif," Sam chimed in. "It's one of my favorites, as a matter of fact."

"Well, it does make sense because many of the doors were used to enclose their granaries. And the grain in the granary feeds the tribal group; in other words, it's nurturing like a mother's milk."

"Let's go to the library/media center and check this stuff out."

We were in agreement and set off for the library and its art books.

CHAPTER FOUR
ABDOULAYE AND AL QAEDA

bdoulaye stopped to get water at a local well. He was by himself. At the last minute, his brother, Senghor, had opted out of the journey. Got cold feet. Abdoulaye had set off by himself for Agadez in Niger. The first stepping stone on the way to Melilla and the Spanish border. He had been on the road alone for a week. So far, so good, except for the fact that he was very thirsty. The central Malian region, *Mopti,* he was passing through was very dry. All around him was scrubby bush. The rain had been very sparse again this year, and he could see the parched crops in the fields as he walked. The harvest might fail again. People were desperate. The very climate itself seemed to have turned against Africa.

He was not only thirsty but hungry, too. However, he needed to conserve his slim resources if he was going to make it straight to cousin Mohamed's house in Agadez with no extra stops. The trip might take two weeks, or it might take a month. He needed to spend as little on food as possible to keep something in reserve. He remembered his last meal of cassava bread longingly.

As he dipped the calabash into the well for another drink, he saw a big cloud of dust down the road. Did he spy flags flying?

"*Merde!*" he said to himself. "*Damn! Who was coming?* It was too quiet here. Where was everyone? *Ils sont où, les villageois?* Where were the villagers?"

Abdoulaye considered trying to hide down inside the well, but that was insanity, so he crouched by the side of the stones and tried to make himself invisible. *Where could he run to?*

Trop tard. Too late. The *quatre-quatres* four-wheel drive vehicles and the motorcycles were upon him. They all screeched to a halt at the well, and his worst fears were realized. The jeeps were flying the black pennants with white Arabic lettering, which meant they were jihadists. Terrorist militants. Six armed men leaped out of the SUV and the battered truck. They wore the uniform of the dreaded Al Qaeda-affiliated group, the *Katibat Macina.*

His heart was literally in his throat. *Maybe they wouldn't see him? Il se faisait petit.* He tried to blend into the side of the well, crouched down out of their sight line.

The jihadists were laughing and talking among themselves. Some were just boys younger than Abdoulaye, but each was armed with a rifle over his shoulder. The teenagers joined up just for the guns and motorbikes they were given to incentivize them. There was one man with a machine gun who was clearly in charge.

"*Fermez-la,*" he commanded imperiously, and the younger soldiers got silent. "*Cherche-moi à boire, toi.*" The youngest soldier, who might have been 11 or 12 years old, hurried to serve his superior with water from the dipper. The older man drank deeply. The troops also drank in turn and started to fill their canteens with water.

Abdoulaye lay absolutely still just feet away from them, his body on the ground curled around the outside edge of the well. He willed himself to disappear into the sandy stones of the coping.

The leader in charge barked out an order, "ça *suffit. Montons!* Get in! We're leaving," and he tossed his last dipper of water on the ground.

Abdoulaye tried not to flinch, but he must have moved. *Putain de merde!* The jig was up. He had given himself away, and they were on him in a second.

"*Qu'est-ce que c'est que ça?*" the head man with a dark beard on his face and white turban on his head jeered at Abdoulaye as two skinny but wiry adolescent soldiers pulled him to his feet.

"A new recruit to the cause? No need to be shy. *Ne sois pas gêné.* We'll be happy to enlist you." They all laughed.

Abdoulaye grimaced. Terrified, he struggled to escape the rough grasp of the boy soldiers holding him on each side. Their grip was like iron. *Je suis foutu*, he thought to himself. *I'm screwed.*

His worst fears had become reality. He had been captured by Islamic revolutionaries. *Were they Dahesh? Were they Salafist jihadists from the FLM, le Front de Libération du Macina?* Abdoulaye had heard of them back in Senegal and their crusade to impose *sharia* law and modes of conduct. *Some were Fulani tribesmen. Dogons? Peu importe.* It mattered little. They would force him to fight for them unless he could escape. *Escape how?*

His body sagged between his two captors. He spit into the dust. His mind was reeling.

"*Tu t'appelles comment?*" the chief asked him.

Abdoulaye choked out his name, "*Abdoulaye.*"

"Louder! *Plus fort!*" the chieftain commanded imperiously. He poked Abdoulaye in the stomach with the business end of his AK 47.

Abdoulaye almost shouted this time, "*je m'appelle Abdoulaye Diop.*"

"Welcome to our happy band. *Bienvenu parmi nous, Abdoulaye,*" the chief teased. All the soldiers laughed again at this clever sally.

"*Je vous ai dit de monter!* I told you to mount up," he barked to the group. They mounted their motorcycles and piled into their vehicles, two of them pushing their captive roughly ahead of them into one of the four-wheel drive trucks.

Tearing over the dusty roads, black pennants flapping in the backdraft, the trucks arrived in a village Abdoulaye later learned was called Moura.

With a nod of his head and a grunt, the commander directed his underlings to throw Abdoulaye in a deep pit "to season him up," so he said.

"*Aie,*" Abdoulaye instinctively cried out in pain as he glanced off the side of the pit and landed with a deafening thud at the bone-dry bottom. He took stock of his injuries. He was bruised, but luckily, he had broken no bones in the fall. *Hmm,* he thought, *I've ended up down a well after all.* His sense of irony had not totally deserted him.

Time passed. Hard to tell how long. He was panicked. He was disoriented. It was totally dark. His head ached, wondering how long they would leave him to stew in here. *What were his chances if he got out? What if he never got out?* He mulled over what he had heard about the situation in Mali over the years and the Islamic terrorists called *Katibat Macina.*

Everyone knew about their commandant, Emir Mahmoud Barry, alias Abou Yehiya, who wanted to bring back the reign of his family through his support of Al Qaeda. He used his men to ruthlessly impose their version of *Sharia* law on the territory they conquered. Then when it suited the politicians in Bamako to make a show for the international community, the FAMA, the Malian government anti-terrorist troops, came to punish Mahmoud Barry's forces using the same brutal methods on the villagers as the terrorists did: arrests based on accusations, summary executions, bodies hastily buried in communal graves, rape, kidnapping, and torture. Unarmed civilians were targeted whether they supported the jihadists or not. It was an endless cycle of violence and retribution for violence.

Wait! What was that noise? Abdoulaye's ears perked up. He was fully alert. *Were his captors coming for him?*

No. It sounded like the *whop, whop, whop* of helicopter blades! Helicopters! *What could they be doing here in the middle of nowhere?*

Abdoulaye felt the ground above him pound with the sound of running feet. Many rounds of staccato gunfire went off. Anguished screams and cries penetrated even down to his underground prison.

More running, screaming, and endless sprays of gunfire. There was the smell of burning. Voices shouted commands in a language he didn't understand.

Something, *a body?* fell with a dull thud at the edge of the pit where he crouched below, trapped. But out of harm's way. A battle seemed to be raging up above in the village.

The noises reached a crescendo, and then the noise of the helicopter blades returned. *Were they departing?*

More time passed. Abdoulaye had dozed off. He awoke with a sickening start, becoming aware of his cramped limbs and desperate situation.

All was quiet above him now. He refused to be buried alive

without a struggle. He stood up and tried to get a handhold or foothold on the smooth sides of the well interior.

He shouted at the top of his lungs in Wolof and in French, *"Au secours! Au secours! Help!"*

He tried to scale the walls again and again. He'd succeed in making a little headway and then would slip back. He was so frustrated and angry that tears welled up in his eyes.

Then, as if his wishing had made it so, a crude ladder appeared and was lowered down into the well.

Abdoulaye took hold of it and nimbly climbed the rungs, blinking like a mole exposed to the sunlight after a long time underground.

A village man, his savior, helped Abdoulaye to climb over the top of the well to freedom. He looked as frightened as Abdoulaye.

"Hélas! Look what they did?," he cried. *"Les salauds! Les fils de pute! C'est atroce.* The murderous bastards! All of them."

He was sobbing with grief and could hardly choke out the words.

"Could you hear them down there? Could you make out what they were saying? I couldn't."

"They were speaking a language I never heard. They were white foreigners. *Bakos. Étrangers.* They came in helicopters. I've heard them called *mercénaires,* 'Wagner' mercenaries, the lowest of the low. And the most bloodthirsty."

"Milice 'Wagner' from Russia?" Abdoulaye said in disbelief.

"They were slaughtering us, killing, shooting, and raping," the villager continued. "What could we poor inhabitants of Moura do against such savagery? We have no weapons. We are farmers, not soldiers of fortune.

Then, the *Katibat* tried to fight the foreigners. Look there on the ground by the well. They killed some of them.

But those radical Islamic dogs are no better than the Wagner forces. They kill, rape, and torture just the same as the soldiers if we don't do as they say. They keep us ignorant. They've closed all the schools! But after today, how many children are left alive anyway?"

The village man's anguish redoubled. *"Mon Dieu, mon Dieu,"* he moaned. *"Allah oma Sa'dnee.* God help us! How can I go on living? How will I not see them, my family, my neighbors—murdered, violated in front of my eyes? How can I not hear their screams?" he sobbed anew.

He was overcome with grief, seeing ghosts with his vacant gaze. He seemed momentarily deranged.

Then, his eyes refocused, and he remembered Abdoulaye standing in front of him.

"Run!" he exhorted the young Senegalese. "Run. I don't know who you are, but you're not one of them, the white devils or the *Katibat.* You're not FAMA, the army, either. I saw the terrorists throw you down there to rot. Run! *Tire-toi!* Save yourself before they come back."

Abdoulaye stood motionless and speechless for a moment, taking in the signs of devastation and mayhem around him. There were fires smoldering, bodies strewn on the ground, contorted and broken. Women and children lay eviscerated by bayonets and bullets.

The smell of recently spilled blood and corpses starting to putrefy in the heat assailed him. Abdoulaye felt nauseated.

He ran for his life.

CHAPTER FIVE

MARIANNE, THE LIBRARIAN

S am and I learned a lot of fascinating information at the Montpezat's *médiathèque,* which lent out books and media like music and film. The 'power figures,' the African wooden statues with nails, razors, and other sharp objects stuck in them, were mostly from the Congo. They had a truth-telling function for a family or tribe. By pounding in a nail, an answer was revealed to a question or problem. Many of these 'truth-telling' sculptures were made in the shape of dogs since dogs could many times sniff out friends from enemies.

A tribal power figure that has proved its value over time as advisor and problem solver is kept in a safe place to be consulted in time of need and as a spirit guardian and lucky talisman for the family or group that owns it.

The stomach area is often hollow and contains roots or special ritual objects. This cavity is sometimes closed by a mirror or other reflective material. It is a form of viewing for spirits of those who have died to see potential enemies or witness transactions in their former community.

"Sam," I said. "I wonder if we can take out some of these books. I'm going to ask at the checkout desk."

"*Certainement*," Sam replied. "Let's see if these art books circulate. Say, isn't that Marianne at the library desk?"

"Why, I believe it is. I wonder what she's doing here."

We lugged a couple of big, heavy art books over to the librarian's post by the door and said hello to Marianne Rambaldini. We knew her as one of the town's biggest *football* supporters.

She was in charge of the soccer team's logistical backup—uniforms, scheduling, transportation, and all the nuts and bolts. She was the wife, or might as well be, of Bruno, an avid *boules* player in town.

Montpezat had a traveling team that had won many lawn bowling or *pétanque* or *boules* tournaments.

Both Marianne and Bruno adored American basketball and never missed an NBA game on television. In fact, they had met playing pick-up basketball in a league in Paris many years ago.

Marianne was much taller than Bruno, but he was well-knit and very athletic.

"Bonjour, Marianne. What are you doing here at the *médiathèque*?" I asked.

"*Bonjour, Barbara, Sam*. Didn't you know? I volunteer here at the *médiathèque* on Sunday mornings. Philippe Hébrard doesn't work on the weekends."

Philippe Hébrard, who lived near us on the main square, was employed by the village to be in charge of the *médiathèque*.

"I guess Philippe Hébrard must be related to our neighbor across the street, René Hébrard," Sam said.

"Oh, no. Not at all," Marianne told us. "Not only aren't they related, but they don't get along at all," she said, leaning in over the desk conspiratorially.

Ok, we thought. *Another little tidbit of village scuttlebutt. We'd better not make assumptions. A lot of the names were the same, but not the political leanings.*

"Marianne, can we check out these big art books?" I asked. "I got a library card a while ago, so I'm on file," I said.

Marianne looked at the book titles. "African Art history," she noticed. "That's interesting. I didn't even know we had these. *Non, désolée,* this kind of reference book cannot be taken home."

"Too bad. *Tant pis.* I suspected as much," I said. "But that's ok; we already found what we were looking for, more or less."

"Well, if you and Sam are interested in Africa, have you heard about the *Africajarc* festival? It's happening soon in the town of Cajarc, about 30 kilometers from here toward St. Cirq laPopie. The whole village of Cajarc does an African-themed weekend," Marianne informed us.

"That sounds different," Sam said. "We'll have to check it out. Maybe you and Bruno would want to come with us, Marianne. What do you think? *Qu'en pensez-vous?*"

"That's a nice idea, Sam. *Merci beaucoup.* I'll have to see if the dates work out with my schedule of soccer matches and Bruno's *boules* meets." Marianne smiled at him.

"Sure," I said. "We'll look into the *Africajarc* schedule and check in with you later."

"*Au revoir.*"

"*Au revoir. Bon appétit.*"

"*Bon appétit.*"

———

It was lunchtime. Walking the short distance back home to have lunch, Sam and I agreed that Marianne was a village treasure. She volunteered for the *football* team and at the *médiathèque*, as we just learned.

She also ran an ad hoc, self-help group for expats and foreigners every Wednesday morning at the *café de l'Union* on the main street. Over cups of coffee, she held informal, very informal, French classes for whoever turned up and advised non-Frenchies where to buy what or how to find what or whoever was needed.

Marianne had grown up in Montpezat. She sometimes took us on walks around the village *chemin de ronde,* the remnants of the medieval battlements. She would point out to us points of local history, like the house which was mistakenly destroyed by the Nazis who mistook it for the Jewish doctor's home.

She remembered the German occupiers from her girlhood. They were the 2nd SS Panzer division, one of the Reich's most brutal units.

In 1944, they were resting in Toulouse and Montauban after months of fighting on the bloody Eastern front.

Ordered to march north to confront the Allies landing in Normandy, they committed atrocities as they marched along. Civilians were hanged and shot in Tulle and Oradour-sur-Glane.

As a reprisal for resistance activity in Montpezat, they locked 15 inhabitants of Perches, a part of the village, in a barn and torched it along with its human contents. Marianne felt that there but for the grace of God and her mother's admonition to get home, she could have been.

She also remembered the house of the people who had diverted Allied funds for the Resistance movement airdropped on the nearby high point at Montalzat. She told us that they kept the money hidden until after the war. Those memories were indelible.

If the old stones of our village could talk, they would have many stories to tell.

CHAPTER SIX

THE AFRICAJARC FESTIVAL

S am and I ended up going to the Africajarc festival by ourselves since Marianne and Bruno were busy that weekend. We drove to the little town of Cajarc on the Saturday evening of the festival to see what there was to see.

Cajarc was a pretty town about 40 minutes to the north of Montpezat. It was in the *Lot* region, just over the border from our *département, le Tarn-et-Garonne.* The signboard said, as we crossed over the border between the two *départements, 'There's a Lot to see in le Lot.'* It was written in *franglais* as a little joke. There were many English people who owned second houses in the region.

Instead of the national highway, we rode on the barely two-lane roads the *Lot* was known for. We passed over the *causse* with its scrubby little oak trees whose roots hid the truffles which grew in the region.

Just before the village of Cajarc, we descended a hill down into the river valley. The light was less intense now, and a faint outline of the moon was visible in the still bright blue sky.

"Why would the village of Cajarc host an African-themed festival each year, I wonder?" Sam asked.

"That is an open question," I said. "I don't really know. It's different from other towns that mostly stage medieval festivals. The French are interested in African culture. They had many former colonies in West Africa, Bénin, Côte d'Ivoire, Cameroon, and, of course, Sénégal. French is still an important second language in those places. I know that Afro-centric music is more popular here than in the US, for example."

"Have you heard of the featured singer at tonight's performance, Barbara?"

"I've heard her on the radio," I answered. "She sings with a group called *Bissa Na Bisso*. *M'Passi* is her name," I said, consulting the festival flier so as to get the names right. "I'm curious to see what she's like in person."

"What else shall we do at the festival?" Sam inquired.

"Well, gosh, I'm not sure. Let's see what's going on when we get to Cajarc. First, we'll have to park, that's for sure."

Sam piloted the Citroën through the winding *rue principale* of Cajarc. It looked quite charming, and we spotted several restaurants and cafés where we could get a bite to eat.

We followed some arrows marked *parking* to a big field where we easily found a spot in a row of other cars.

I found it surprising and appealing that no matter how crowded the venue, people in France stayed calm and unhurried. There was no angst or pushing to get ahead in line or rush to reserve a seat.

We got out of the car and followed some more arrows marked *festival* for a short way to a kind of tent city with a bunch of stalls selling African-themed objects of all shapes, sizes, and descriptions.

There were the usual baskets and drums, beads and

trinkets, canes and letter openers with carved heads, piles of African fabrics like kente cloth, mud cloth prints, and the scratchy raffia fabric, Kuba cloth, which was my favorite.

I admired the amazing colors and daring designs of the cotton wax prints on display. The creativity of their color juxtapositions seemed endless. Whether the cottons were printed with abstract designs, leaf patterns, or airplanes, they were fabulously bold.

Sam's eye was attracted by an odd-shaped, dark wooden object among the sculptures in a booth. It was a semi-circular section of hoop supported on a two-legged stand. The hoop section was about 10 inches long and 2 inches wide. The legs held it 6 inches off the table.

We stopped to examine it, and the Frenchman tending the stall approached us.

"Interesting, isn't it? Do you know what it is?"

"No idea," Sam said. "Isn't it a sculpture?"

"No, not exactly," the vendor replied. "It's a headrest, in other words, a pillow."

"That is unusual. It looks unlike any pillow I ever saw," Sam exclaimed.

"Quite so," the vendor said. "In hot weather climates like Africa, a feather or foam pillow would be too hot under the head. This little object, on the other hand, elevates the head a little off the ground but keeps the air circulating around it."

"It is handsome. It could be a sculpture with its simple, pure lines," Sam persisted.

"Of course, you're very right," agreed the stall owner. "This example is handsome for its simple, spare lines. The Zulu people, on the other hand, make very decorated, sculptural headrests on the same principle as this one to protect their elaborate hairstyles while they sleep."

"I really like it. How much is it?" Sam asked the man. "What do you think of it, Barbara?"

"I like it too, Sam. You've certainly got an eye. I think it would look great up on the fireplace mantle added to our collection of objects on display."

So Sam negotiated a bit on the asking price, which wasn't too high to begin with. We became the proud owners of a wooden pillow slash African sculpture. The seller happily gave us change for our 30 euros and his card with his name written on it: *François Lamy, dealer in Africana, artifacts, and arcana.*

I looked at him and his card. They were both a little wrinkled and worse for the wear.

"Monsieur Lamy," I asked him, "have you been dealing in African objects for quite a while now?"

François Lamy answered that he had been fascinated by African art objects since he was a boy and had made many trips to the African continent to study and collect.

"Have you ever sold any 'power figures,' the statues with nails?" I asked him. "Do you know anything about them?"

"Aha, Madame. Could you be thinking about the 'power figure' statuette that recently went missing from the restaurant in Caussade, by any chance?"

"Yes, as a matter of fact," I told him. "I am fascinated by that sculpture. We happened to be dining at *La Table d'Alice* the very night of the theft and the attempted kidnapping. They say the statue might have been taken during all the commotion. Did you read about it?"

"Yes, I've been following the story very closely. You see, that statuette was a well-known *N'Kisi Kongo* figure. *N'Kisi* means male. Some power figures are female.

It was the property of the Kongo people, who have been

seeking its repatriation for some time now. They say it was spirited away from them by missionaries in the 19th century.

Now that the Chinese have built a state-of-the-art museum in Kinshasa, the capital of the Democratic Republic of the Congo, they feel it should be returned to Africa where it can be just as well preserved as in Europe."

"Did it belong to Alice, the restaurant owner?" I asked the art dealer.

"That is a long story, Madame. Please stop by later or give me a call. You have the telephone number on my card."

"Of course," I said. "I can see that you're busy now." Other potential buyers were perusing the wares on François Lamy's table.

Sam and I moved off, carrying the plastic bag containing his purchase.

We headed away down the row of other displays, looking for the music venue. We found the big stage, spread out the blanket we brought for the purpose, and sat down on the grass with lots of other people to wait for the start of the show.

"Maybe I'll call him sometime. What do you think?" I asked Sam.

"You mean the sculpture seller?" Sam said. "Yes, sure. It would be interesting to follow up on what he knows about the 'power figure.' The attempted kidnapping and the whole affair seem to have disappeared from the news."

The footlights of the stage lit up.

"Look, the show is starting."

The performers came out on the stage with a flourish, pulsing with energy. The six members of the *Bissa Na Bisso* group were rappers. They rapped in French and Yoruba, a Nigerian language.

Rap music was not my favorite genre, but the group was

tuneful, and the French lyrics, which I could make out, were clever rhymes and not violent.

Then, the five male members of the rap group faded into the wings, leaving M'Passi, the sole young woman on stage. She started to sing, and Sam and I were carried away with admiration for her sweet, throaty voice.

I had expected something more hard-driving, but M'Passi sang lovely, jazzy ballads in her mellow voice. She reminded me of the singer Nora Jones, Ravi Shankar's daughter.

We leaned back on our blanket under the stars and totally enjoyed the music. It was exotic yet accessible. She even sang a rendition of "Hakuna Matata" from *The Lion King*.

Lovely M'Passi had the audience under her musical spell for the rest of the performance. It set the tone for the remainder of our Africajarc outing and lingered in the back of our minds as we drove back to Montpezat later that night.

CHAPTER SEVEN

AGADEZ, NIGER

Abdoulaye Diop had been fortunate. He had made it overland to his cousin's house in Agadez in the very north of Niger without further incident. True, he was alone since his brother, Senghor, had lost heart and opted to stay back in Senegal.

For a brief, scary time in Mali, Abdoulaye thought his younger brother had made the right choice. Abdoulaye's close call with the Islamic terrorists had been terrifying. After a week of walking and hitchhiking across Mali, the young man had almost been conscripted into the *Katibat Macina* fighting there. He had just managed to escape with his life. But he was young, strong, and had a positive outlook.

When he reached Mohamed's modest concrete block house, he was feeling fine—happy and proud of himself. Step one on the journey to Europe was now accomplished. Mohamed, his cousin, was overjoyed to see him appear safe and sound in his village on the edge of town.

"Abdoulaye! *Mon cher cousin!* Let me look at you. You are

a grown man since I saw you last. Where is Senghor? Is he alright? Are you alright?"

Abdoulaye explained about Senghor's defection. His feelings were still hurt, but each person must make their own decision before undertaking such a dangerous trip as the one he was setting out on.

He embraced cousin Mohamed, who was anxious to hear all the news of their family back in Senegal.

Mohammed's dwelling was very basic, but there was always room to roll out some more bedding on his floor. He was happy to let Abdoulaye stay with him for a while to regain his full strength after the rigors of his journey and his run-in with the Islamic terrorists in Mali.

His horrific experience had not dampened his fighting spirit. If anything, the hard trip had made Abdoulaye stronger and more determined.

There was already another visitor who occupied one corner of the main room, a young man of about Abdoulaye's age. They even resembled one another, but Abdoulaye had grown a short beard during his travels, and the other young man was clean-shaven.

Over a meal of *poulet yassa*, Senegalese chicken with onions and lemon, and *fufu*, Malian mashed plantains, Abdoulaye learned that his fellow wayfarer was a Nigerian from down south near the Niger River delta.

The man's name was Ekon Ibrahim. He wasn't in the best of health. He was plagued by an infection on his lower leg, which wouldn't seem to heal despite the herb poultice Mohamed's wife had prepared for him to apply to the wound.

The visitors got down to exchanging stories of their respective odysseys. Abdoulaye explained the plight which had impelled him to search for a new life far away from his country.

He told Ekon that the fishing economy off of Saint Louis had been decimated first by rising sea levels, which had forced his family to flee inland, and then by foreign trawlers that scooped up the lion's share of the deep water catch.

"And now," he continued, "there is talk of a big natural gas discovery off Senegal's shores toward Mauritania."

He continued, warming to his subject, "Perhaps the gas discovery will benefit Saint Louis eventually. That's what the officials say. But in the meantime, the zone of the gas exploitation will further reduce the legal fishing area."

Ekon nodded sympathetically. "I understand all too well. My story is similar to yours, but where I lived in Nigeria, we have already suffered disastrous effects from oil and gas exploration and drilling. Our fishing industry was decimated. Our fields were polluted with oil runoff and noxious chemical fumes. We also were promised jobs in the new industry, but my people, the *Ogoni*, are simple folk, not engineers. It pains me to say it, but I think you made the right choice to flee while you're still young and strong."

Ekon Ibrahim went on citing facts and figures. He explained that as of 2020, African migrants made up 15% of the global migrant population, compared to Europe's 22% and Asia's 41%. But less than a third of all African migrants lived in Europe. They migrated within Africa. Some were pushed by unpredictable weather patterns across the African region, which sent people from other poorer and less stable African countries to Senegal.

Ekon said, "You are fleeing from Senegal. Yet Senegal's open borders pull other people into the country. Climate change forces West Africans, most of whom do agriculture, to migrate as a coping strategy. Poverty is relative, and life in

Senegal, difficult though it may be, is easier than in other parts of Africa."

He cited as an example his own area in the Niger River Delta, where he told Abdoulaye that the native Ogoni tribal people were destitute.

Ekon seemed stronger and more authoritative when he started talking like this. He had a lot of facts and figures on the tip of his tongue. His weakened physical condition had disguised his education and expertise. Now that he had got started, he got carried away, talking in his charismatic way.

He explained how his people, the Ogoni tribe, had been duped and dumped upon by the international oil companies and their own Nigerian politicians for fifty years.

Their land, and the land of all the peoples in the Nigerian delta region, had been savaged, and their livelihoods destroyed.

They had never benefited in the slightest way from the billions of dollars in oil and gas riches pumped out of their territory. All this profit had gone to the international oil companies Shell and Chevron in a joint venture with the NNPC.

"What is the NNPC?" Abdoulaye asked.

Ekon replied that the letters stood for the Nigerian National Petroleum Corporation. He felt strongly that the NNPC was a conduit to siphon off money to Nigerian officials who lived in the north of the country and completely neglected the south.

Yet without the oil revenue that did get reported and used to repay the World Bank, Nigeria as a country would be insolvent.

Despite lip service and a few programs put in place to help the Ogoni River people, the Delta region had never benefited from the tremendous wealth it had created for others.

Ekon Ibrahim proudly asserted that he was fighting to change this lamentable state of affairs. He recounted how he had formed an alliance with other Ogoni tribesmen who were as fed up as he was.

They were inspired by an organization called MOSOP, the Movement for the Survival of the Ogoni People, whose leader was Ken Saro-Wiwa. Before MOSOP's leadership was eliminated by its enemies, the organization had made strides toward getting fairer treatment for the Delta region.

MOSOP demonstrators had stood in front of the oil rigs. Their activists had interrupted drilling operations. Other members had besieged the government ministries in the capital cities of Nigeria, Abuja and Lagos, shouting slogans and waving banners.

The entrenched interests, the foreign oil companies, and the corrupt politicians—their own countrymen—who were in their pockets tried to ignore MOSOP.

In spite of attempts to stop it, MOSOP had success publicizing the cause. The opposition reacted violently. MOSOP members were threatened verbally and then physically attacked.

Abdoulaye was enrapt listening to Ekon's tale. The young Ogoni's voice shook with emotion as he recounted how villages in the Delta region were burned, women raped, and people displaced and murdered in an effort to suppress the movement.

MOSOP's leader, Ken Saro-Wiwa, was a well-known and respected Nigerian writer, as well as an activist. The government of Nigeria executed him and seven other supposed MOSOP conspirators by hanging in 1994. They were arrested and condemned to death after the speediest show trial in Nigerian history, a trial which the UN observers called a setup and a travesty of justice.

Ekon went on, fired up with his cause, "It is my goal to improve the lot of the Ogoni. I want to take up the fight for our rights the way Ken Saro Wiwa and MOSOP did. The despoliation of our land cannot go on."

What an account! It was horrific. The injustice of it all was crushing.

Abdoulaye asked, "How is it that I never heard of the Ogoni or these injustices in the Niger Delta? A show trial! Sentences of hanging! The UN knew about it?"

Ekon elaborated, "Well, there were UN observers to the executions, but they could do nothing but register a protest. There was an outcry in the United States, but the Americans buy 35% of Nigeria's oil output. They have a vested interest in the status quo. The shame, the great shame of it, is that it is still going on. Nothing has changed. The northern Hausa, the Yoruba, and Igbo peoples who control Nigeria are still raping my people."

Abdoulaye was very impressed by Ekon's recitation. His reaction was immediate. "Why, this makes my blood boil! How could this be allowed to happen? This is what might happen to us in Senegal! Did you know about this, cousin Mohamed?" Abdoulaye asked their host, who had also been listening to Ekon's diatribe.

Mohamed replied, "Yes, I was more or less *au courant*. You two were very young when all this happened in the 1990s. I'm older than you and Ekon, so I was aware of the MOSOP movement and its brutal suppression. The show trial and the hangings scared people into silence." And then, "I now live in Niger, way north of the delta oil fields. Niger has its own problems and injustices aplenty."

Mohamed went over and sat on a stool near Ekon. The two bent their heads together in quiet conversation. Mohamed seemed to be encouraging Ekon to do something, and Ekon seemed hesitant.

Mohamed spoke first. "Abdoulaye, please listen. Ekon Ibrahim has something to ask you. It is of very great importance to him and his people. Please weigh what he has to tell you with the utmost seriousness. The outcome of many lives, including your own, could depend upon your response to what he has to say."

CHAPTER EIGHT

LUNCH WITH THE AFRICAN ART SELLER

Back in the *Tarn-et-Garonne,* Sam and I arranged to have lunch with François Lamy, the Africana expert, at *La Table d'Alice.* The tables outside around the patio were mostly occupied, which suited our purpose.

We asked Édouard, Alice's husband, to seat us inside the restaurant near the African sculpture with the nails in its stomach. That way, our art dealer acquaintance could study it without attracting too much attention, and our conversation would not be overheard. We wanted him to see the more modern interpretation of a 'power figure' before the restaurant installed a new art exhibition, as they did every two months or so.

As we settled in at our table, putting our napkins on our laps, our art dealer acquaintance could barely control his indignation and admiration.

"This carving and the majority of these examples come from the heart of Africa, an area which was formerly called the Congo in the colonial era," François Lamy said. "Did you know that at the present time, there are two Congos, two countries with similar names separated by the Congo River?"

Sam and I shook our heads. Neither one of us knew very much about the geography of Africa.

Lamy continued, "Yes, you see, there are the former Belgian colony, the Democratic Republic of Congo, on one side of the river and the much smaller Republic of the Congo just on the other bank."

Turning his attention back to the N'Kisi carving on the pedestal next to our table, he continued. "I don't have to look very closely to see that this statue is a crude but cunning imitation of the real thing. There should never be nails in the stomach since the stomach was the vessel containing medicinal matter that originally attracted the spiritual forces of the figure."

François Lamy became very solemn and said, stressing his words, "The stomach area of the authentic Congolese power figures is always left hollow to hold the precious relics, herbs, or bone that endow the statue with its magical force to sense and eliminate evil.

The crevice in the power figure's stomach area is often covered with a reflective material to protect the charms and to illustrate how the N'Kisi can 'see' into the past and the future."

With a wave of his hand, the art dealer indicated the recently carved N'Kisi figure on the pedestal next to our table and said with disdain, "There should never be nails in the stomach like there are in this example here. Furthermore, these nails seem to form some kind of a pattern. That is not as one would expect. However, in some respects, it is very nicely executed," he admitted grudgingly.

M. Lamy was certainly well-informed. I noticed how his

eyes glinted in an acquisitive, hostile way when he looked at the modern statuette standing innocently on its pedestal.

I was perplexed by his malevolent glances in the statue's direction. It was as if he couldn't wait to get his hands on it and wrest something out of it.

I supposed that as an African antique dealer and expert, he must have something against this copy of the real McCoy and yet want to acquire it at the same time. It seemed contradictory.

"Do you see the carving's raised right fist and the angry facial expression?" Francois Lamy said with a loud growl as if imitating what the statuette might sound like.

"Shhh, Monsieur Lamy. *Chut, s'il vous plaît,*" we shushed him. "That's quite interesting, but we don't want to call attention to ourselves."

Lamy got himself under control and quieted down.

"What were the nails for?" Sam asked in a low voice.

"The function of the nails is to document vows sealed, treaties signed, and efforts to eradicate evil." Lamy lectured us.

"The metals in an authentic statue attest to its role as witness and enforcer of matters of crucial importance to its community. A peg driven into a statue represents a matter that has been settled. A nail implies a more serious situation, such as a murder. Driving objects into the statue made it angry, so it began to take action."

"Is that why it looks so angry?" I inquired. "Because it was hurt by the nails?"

"No. The facial expressions in 'power figures' are carved to appear menacing in order to intimidate potential enemies. They also are made to encourage potential evil-doers to think twice about the consequences they will suffer if they violate established codes of social conduct."

Having said this, the Africana dealer became very quiet.

By chance, our lunch was served right then. We all dug into big salad plates of *melons du Quercy* wrapped with Serrano ham.

The atmosphere lightened again. M. Lamy seemed more at ease, so we continued to pick his brain.

We wanted to know if, by any chance, he knew who owned the stolen statuette. And he did! Lamy told us that the authentic *N'Kisi Kongo* 'power figure' was the property of an elderly ex-governor general of the former colony of Nigeria.

It transpired that this former military officer had retired to our area, the *Tarn-et-Garonne,* after his long, distinguished career in the Queen's overseas government. It was rumored that he intended to return the statuette to its tribal owners at his death, but since he was British, it might also be donated to the British Museum in London instead.

By the time we were selecting our dessert of homemade sorbets—*mangue,* mango, *cassis,* black currant or *fruit de la passion,* passion fruit—Sam and I had gleaned a lot of information. We learned that by warping the original intent of the *N'Kisi Kongo* 'power figures' and Haitian vodou practices, Hollywood had created modern-day stick-pin voodoo dolls that sometimes appear in movies.

Ha! That was funny to think about, but it made sense.

"Monsieur Lamy," I asked, "I can see why someone might have taken the real power figure to sell or even to give back to its original tribal owners, but why bother to fabricate this modern figure with nails where there aren't usually any? Do you have any ideas about that?"

Sam poured the last of the *vin rosé des Côteaux du Quercy* from the *pichet,* or pitcher, we had ordered into M. Lamy's glass. Lamy considered the question for a while, sipping at his wine.

"Non, aucune idée," he finally said unhelpfully. "I have no idea. But I do now recall the name of the ex-governor general of Nigeria. He's called the Right Honorable Sir Hiram Pickett-Smythe. And I think he lives in your sector, around Montpezat de Quercy, if I'm not mistaken. The old gent must be in his nineties if he's a day."

At this moment, Alice came into the dining room. She was holding her son, Manu, by the hand. The little boy looked very happy. He was smiling sweetly as his mother led him along. They both seemed to be completely recovered from the frightening abduction incident.

As they approached our table, Monsieur Lamy suddenly announced, "And now I must be going. Thank you very kindly for lunch. *Merci infiniment.*" He excused himself and ducked quickly away from our table. With a little inclination of the head, he was out the door.

Sam and I asked for *l'addition,* the bill, which we paid, and then we also went on our way.

"That Monsieur Lamy sure made a fast getaway when it was time to pay the bill," Sam said as we climbed into the car. "He's a slippery one if you ask me."

I couldn't help but agree with Sam. There was something that didn't add up about our luncheon partner, alright. He was so intense, almost obsessed with these African objects. Occupational hazard, I guessed.

"Yes, Lamy certainly has mastered the art of sticking others with the bill," I laughed ruefully. "But I did invite him after all."

"You know, Sam, I've been thinking," I said as we drove along the D820 toward Montpezat and home.

"Uh oh," Sam laughed. "When are you not thinking? What's on your mind now?"

"Well, don't laugh at me, but you know that old English gentleman who walks in la rue de la Libération on market days? The one with his slightly younger French companion?"

"I think I know who you mean. You've mentioned them before, but I never paid too much attention."

"Yes," I continued. "The old Englishman found out one time that we live in Florida in the winter, and now whenever I see him, he asks me about Jacksonville."

"Jacksonville, but we don't live anywhere near Jacksonville," Sam replied quizzically.

"No, we don't, but this old guy is very interested in the composer, Delius, who composed a piece of music on the theme of the St. Johns River in Jacksonville. He's a very cultivated chap. Not Delius, but the old man.

He always asks me if I've listened to it. He's very sweet, leaning on his cane with his straw fedora in his hand. He's quite distinguished in a frail way. You can still see traces of his military bearing."

"Okay," Sam said. "I see where you're going with this. You think that maybe this old gentleman with upper-class English manners is possibly our ex-governor general of Nigeria. Am I right?"

"Well, it's just a possibility. Stranger things have happened. I'm going to ask him more about himself the next time we have our chat about the St. Johns River and Delius."

———

The summer months passed by pleasantly. Sam and I got involved in our usual round of activities, taking excursions to surrounding towns and having aperitif hours and dinners with our neighbors. I never did have further opportunity to talk with our elderly British neighbor. I didn't run into him at the Saturday market or strolling around town with his lady friend.

Sam and I were busy and preoccupied with our daily lives. African 'power figures' and former British governors of African colonies got relegated to the back burner.

CHAPTER NINE

THE MAP, KEY TO AN AFRICAN OIL STRIKE

B ack in Niger at the house in Agadez, Ekon Ibrahim cleared his throat and adjusted the bandages on his leg. He asked Abdoulaye and cousin Mohamed to pray. They faced east on their mats and bowed to Allah, asking his blessing.

Prayers accomplished, the Ogoni activist then removed a small piece of paper from between the pages of the Quran lying next to him and showed it to Abdoulaye and Mohamed. In size, it resembled one of the book's small pages. It had been plasticized to protect it.

Ekon Ibrahim cleared his throat and announced portentously, "I have something very precious here with me. It is the key to a fabulous oil field discovery offshore in the Niger River Delta region. This map I hold in my hand shows the location of a new oil field that promises to be even richer than the Agbami field, the richest strike ever discovered on Ogoni territory up to now!" Ekon beamed triumphantly as he held the plastic-coated paper out for their inspection.

Ekon Ibrahim explained that the map was a section of a geological survey that had no value by itself. To decipher the oil deposit's location, the map had to be combined with its counterpart, a *N'Kisi Kongo* 'power figure.' A replica of a 'power figure' statue had been specially designed so that the pattern of its nails matched up with the map's markings. When the map was placed in the correct orientation over the nails in the statue's stomach, the longest nail would point directly to the coordinates of the undersea oil field.

The young Ogoni man's voice fell into a lower register. "Unfortunately, as you have perhaps sensed, I am not well. I cannot deliver the map to Europe and find the statue by myself any longer. I must entrust this job to others."

"The replica N'Kisi Kongo statuette is in Europe, not in Africa?" Abdoulaye asked.

Ekon replied, "Yes, that's right. In the corrupt political and economic environment of my country, yes, we had to take the necessary steps to hide this fabulous discovery. The statuette was smuggled out of Africa and taken to France by a trusted friend who knows all about the Ogoni and is sympathetic to our cause. He was an oil engineer himself. His name is Édouard Blancpain."

"Édouard Blancpain!" Abdoulaye cried out in surprise. "Why, that's the name of my half-sister's French husband. Your statue is in France with Alice and her husband?"

Abdoulaye's cousin Mohammed, who had been quiet listening to this dialogue, spoke up at this juncture.

"Cousin, it is not entirely by chance that you have met Ekon Ibrahim at my house in Agadez. When I learned that you were heading here to spell your attempt to get to Melilla and then to Spain, I contacted him."

"You contacted him because I was coming here?"

Abdoulaye remarked. "Who am I to him? I am one of many thousands of poor migrants who have a small chance of making it alive across the Mediterranean Sea, let alone finding an African statue."

"Very true, very true, Abdoulaye," Ekon intoned sagely. "But you do have *un atout*, an ace in your hand that few others can claim. You are related to Alice Blancpain, *n'est-ce pas?* Your half-sister, Alice, is married to Édouard Blancpain, the man who possesses the statuette that is the reciprocal part of the key to the map. Édouard was formerly a high-ranking oil company executive in Nigeria. He saw firsthand how the Ogoni have been robbed and maltreated, and he is determined to help us."

Abdoulaye began to get the picture and said, "You are correct. I was planning to contact Alice and her husband for help as soon as I arrived in mainland Europe. But I still have no way of getting there, to the mainland. How are you going to solve that problem?"

Ekon Ibrahim, Abdoulaye's counterpart in age and looks, smiled at his young Senegalese look-alike.

"I think I have a solution for you, my friend. I was to be met at the border crossing at Melilla, and the fix was in. The authorities will let me or someone they assume to be me pass through the frontier.

You will take my identity but not my infirmities. In return for this help, you will deliver the map into the hands of your half-sister's husband, whom you were intending to contact in any case."

"That sounds too good to be true," said Abdoulaye. "What's the catch?"

"Eh bien, Abdoulaye, c'est comme ça," Ekon Ibrahim explained to the man to whom he was now entrusting his hopes

for the betterment of his tribe: "Do you see the injury on my leg here? I was held up by a knife-wielding stranger who tried to rob me. Coincidence? I doubt it. I suspected that I was being followed for some time. The man pinned me against a wall to search me. I was able to break away with the last of my strength, but not before he cut my ankle down to the bone. If you accept to transport the oil field map to France, you will have to be on your guard against people who will stop at nothing to steal it from you."

Abdoulaye had another question. "But Ekon, a statue and a map, these methods are so old-fashioned. Statuettes with nails? Treasure maps? Why don't you use high-tech methods to get the information out?"

"That is a good question," Ekon agreed. "We decided that we would have a better chance of success in preventing our enemies from stealing the oil deposit's location by using precisely these old-fashioned methods. The oil companies and the Nigerian government have many spies well-versed in the latest technology. My tribe is hoping to put them off the scent by going below the technological radar, so to speak."

Ekon's voice swelled with emotion. "This information is so sought after that word of the discovery has gotten out, and I fear our efforts may be foiled if we do not transfer the information soon. Others are trying to get to the oil field first.

That is where you come in. We can't allow this enormous bonanza to pass us by. This oil strike could mean redemption for my people."

Watching Abdoulaye closely to gauge his reaction to this information, Ekon said, "Please, hold the map in your hand." With that, he placed the geological survey into Abdoulaye's open palm.

"Take a good look at what I'm talking about. This is the precious key to unlock the flow of riches that will mean prosperity for my people."

Abdoulaye studied the small piece of plasticized map he held in his hand. It looked innocuous enough.

The Ogoni continued with his instructions: "Your responsibility will have ended only when you have safely delivered it into the very hands of Édouard Blancpain, your half-sister's husband, none other. He will know how to align the map's coordinates with the nails in the N'Kisi Kongo statue in his possession.

Once he has pinpointed the drilling site, he will communicate with our tribal ruler, King Emere. The king, his team of geologists, and their consortium of investors can then start to build the platforms that will start the flow of oil. The oil profits will pay to reverse the ecological damage done to our lands and waters. The oil revenue will pay for our tribe to become educated engineers and businesspeople, the future directors of the future OPC, the Ogoni Petroleum Company."

Incroyable! Incredible. Abdoulaye sat quietly for several minutes, a bit stunned, letting it all sink in.

"*Eh bien,* what do you say?" Ekon Ibrahim asked.

"*D'accord. Je comprends.* I accept the mission and the risks," the young Senegalese man answered with the supreme confidence of youth. "And you will help me get to France to make this delivery?" Abdoulaye inquired. "Just how will that be arranged?"

Ekon, who was enormously pleased by Abdoublaye's acceptance of the deal, took back the map and put it away for safekeeping. "Let us explain to you how it will work."

It was Mohamed who took over. "MOSOP, the Movement for the Survival of the Ogoni People, has connections with the

Moroccans at Melilla, which will allow a certain Ekon Ibrahim to pass through the border crossing into Spain. You will assume Ekon's identity by taking his *laissez-passer* visa documentation and present it to the border police authorities at the gates in the walls at the frontier."

"And once I am admitted to Melilla? What do I do then?" Abdoulaye asked, trying to play it cool and not betray his excitement at this incredible turn of events, which would solve the problem of how he might get onto European territory.

Ekon picked up the narrative and said, "Nothing more complicated than getting yourself, or rather yourself as my alter ego, to the Migrant Help Center where you will be required to take a health examination and fill out your request for asylum. Your near-death experience with the *Katibat Macina,* the homegrown branch of Al Qaeda in Mali, should qualify you for protection. Furthermore, the latest EU regulations give priority to young people willing to work in construction and in the restaurant industry. There is presently a big shortage of this kind of manpower in the European Union.

After a two-week wait for processing time, if all goes as planned, the Spanish authorities may take you to Madrid. From there, you can contact your half-sister, Alice, in France and make your way to her and the statuette."

MADRID! Abdoulaye thought to himself in capital letters. *With a work VISA! This would be the fulfillment of his dream! From Spain, he could make his way to France and find Alice and Édouard, deliver the map, and get on with his new life in Europe.*

Ekon Ibrahim watched the successive reactions on Abdoulaye's face as he digested this information. His eyes shining with joy, the young Senegalese turned to the Ogoni to give his eager accord to the plan.

"Before you thank me, Abdoulaye, remember that this scrap of paper, which is your ticket to the European Union, is from now on your most precious possession. You need to protect it. I have been tracked and spied upon by agents trying to get their hands on it, just as there have been attempts to steal the corresponding N'Kisi Kongo statuette from Édouard Blancpain in France. You must be on your guard at all times in case our opponents from the Nigerian National Petroleum Company or Chevron Oil are looking for me at the border and have bought off the border guards to prevent my passage."

"When do I leave?" Abdoulaye wanted to know. The less time lost, the better, they all agreed.

CHAPTER TEN

DESTINATION MOROCCO

F rom Agadez, Abdoulaye Diop was on the move. The very next morning, he waved farewell to his cousin and the cousin's Ogoni visitor as he set off for the Algerian border on his way to Melilla, that little bit of Europe clinging to the African continent at the edge of Morocco.

His cousin, Mohammed, and especially Ekon Ibrahim, clasped him around the shoulders in a strong embrace and gave him an emotional send-off. They watched for a while as his young, well-built figure retreated along the dusty road that headed north toward the border with Algeria.

Abdoulaye was leaving Mohamed's house with no more than the clothes on his back, some provisions in a small backpack, and enough West African CFA francs (each worth .0016 US dollars) to try to make it into Algeria.

The precious map of the oil deposit to take to France was sewn into a secret pocket in the rear pocket of his tattered pants.

The *laissez-passer* document, which said that his name was Ekon Ibrahim, was secreted in his backpack to be at the ready when he eventually reached the Spanish border at Melilla.

Abdoulaye had shaved off his scrap of beard, which made his resemblance to Ekon Ibrahim even more pronounced.

He was also wearing a braided bracelet, strung with beads in the Ogoni tribe's colors of blue, yellow, and green, on his left wrist. Ekon had removed it from his own arm and gifted it to him at the last minute—a good luck charm and a reminder of the Ogoni cause.

The young man was happy to be on the road again. He felt a strong surge of optimism as he walked along, half-heartedly trying to thumb a ride on one of the passing lorries that rumbled by from time to time. It was unlikely anyone would pick him up.

Truck drivers between Niger and Algeria never transported hitchhikers because they had to pass along routes controlled by successive checkpoints. Smuggling migrants wasn't worth being arrested or having one's vehicle seized.

Abdoulaye was on foot heading for the nearest border town to Algeria. From there, he needed to get to the town of Tamanrasset, a transit point from Niger into Algeria from time immemorial. He was following an ancient camel caravan route controlled and run by the Tuareg tribe.

These nomadic people moved their herds of sheep and goats ceaselessly around this region just south of the Sahara desert, *le Sahel*.

The French colonizers thought of the Tuareg tribe as the 'blue men' because the indigo clothes and scarves they wore around their faces and heads dyed their skin a deep blue. Romantic legends swirled about them.

At one time, the smuggling of goods and people across the Mali-Niger border into Algeria was a thriving industry that benefited everyone on all sides of the frontier. But no longer.

This region of northern Mali and western Niger had become a war zone, and the Tuareg had taken up arms. They were fighting Al Qaeda militant forces led by a fearsome Islamic Jihad leader from Mali—Iyad Ag Ghali. His army prowled the desert, trying to impose fundamentalist *Sharia* law on the Tuareg.

Al Qaeda had almost succeeded in destroying their more moderate Islamic way of life. To gain control, the jihadists burned the ancient manuscripts for which the region was famous and dynamited ancient Unesco Heritage sites, the adobe mosques, and mausoleums, enslaving the people of the region's big cities like Timbuktu and Gao.

The Tuareg were also fighting for independence from the central government, which had left them prey to Al Qaeda militant forces for two long, bloody years.

Neither the Mali central government in Bamako nor the French Barkhane army forces who nominally patrolled the Azawad region interceded on their behalf until 2022.

And now the French troops had pulled out entirely.

If you factored in the sustained drought conditions of recent years to these armed uprisings, you had the recipe for a maelstrom of troubles.

The Azawad region of northern Mali and northwest Niger had become a transit point, dangerous though it was, for people fleeing north from the insecurity and climate change which plagued many Africans living farther south and west in Nigeria and Senegal.

These migrants, like Abdoulaye, were headed for Algeria as a staging point to Europe.

Algeria was resentful at being forced by its location to be the unwilling gatekeeper for the European countries. Overwhelmed and unable to accommodate the flow of people wishing to transit through its territory, Algeria had now closed its border to the influx of thousands of refugees seeking a passage to the Mediterranean and on to the holy grail, the European mainland.

Abdoulaye joined the rest of the human tide headed for the border crossing into Algeria from Niger.

Once he arrived near the border, he would need to find a *coxeur,* a people smuggler, to get him across. From there, he would traverse the length of Algeria and a bit of Morocco before arriving at Melilla's border.

As he walked steadily onward for ten days, he made good time. His luck held. He made it through this minefield of armed militias, each trying to eradicate and subjugate the others, and arrived at the nearest border town unmolested and unscathed.

He stayed there for a month, sleeping on the sand and earning money loading Algerian semolina into trucks. He used the cash he made to buy food and saved up to eventually pay a smuggler to help him cross the border.

Asking around, he met Samir, a Tuareg who ran an informal people transit service with his cousin based in Algeria. When Samir regrouped a few migrants in northern Niger seeking to move across the border, he communicated via *WhatsApp?* with his cousin in Tamanrasset and fixed a GPS point around 25 km outside the border crossing at night.

Right now, Samir said that border monitoring was high and the people movers should wait for a better opportunity.

This gave Abdoulaye some more time to get together enough money to pay the around 8000 DZD, Algerian dinars, or 60 US dollars demanded by Samir. Samir and his cousin could earn up to 70,000 DZD (US$500) per trip smuggling migrants across the border. This made it well worth their while to take the risk of avoiding the frequent patrols from the Algerian side.

On the chosen night, Abdoulaye and his fellow human cargo were deposited in total darkness in the desert about 2 kilometers from the Algerian border. They had expected to be escorted to the crossing point by Samir, but instead, they were dropped off in the sand dunes and simply pointed in the general direction of the distant frontier.

Abdoulaye and some others ran as fast as they could to cover the ground, praying they were headed the right way.

Then, they were met by a surprise obstacle, a huge sand berm created to block their passage into Algeria.

Abdoulaye had heard about the sand berm, but he had not expected the climb to be so long and arduous. He felt exposed to border patrols and their long-range rifles every step of the way. To his relief, he made it to the other side and found himself across the border in Algeria, but where to go from there?

Samir, the *coxeur,* was not there to meet him as agreed upon on this side of the border. He had no choice but to struggle ahead a few more kilometers in the cold and dark of the desert night, shivering from fear and the intense cold. Wrung out and exhausted, he stumbled into Tamanrasset, where instead of finding a place to rest and restore himself, he was instead buttonholed by the same Samir who had let him down.

The smuggler demanded another 15 euros to help Abdoulaye to get one step further.

Since he had no more money, his contract was sold to a friend of Samir's, and he spent the next three months carrying boxes in El Akla, a nearby Algerian market town. He had no choice but to submit to this blackmail.

All in all, Abdoulaye considered himself lucky not to have undergone worse exploitation. Some migrants were attacked and killed by bandits as they made their way through the desert and over the berm at the frontier. Some died of exposure. Women and children were particularly vulnerable to being sold into servitude or sexual slavery until such time as their smugglers claimed that they had worked off the price of their passage. Money transfer shakedown schemes proliferated. Families back home were coerced into wiring money via the *Orange Money* app for their relatives' release.

Finally, after having purged his phony debt, Abdoulaye was driven north to the city of Nador in Morocco, just ten kilometers outside of his goal, Melilla. He was dropped off in a forested area of Mount Gourougou, which was a staging point for migrants waiting for admission to the Spanish side of the wall or hoping to find an illegal entry point to Melilla by sea.

At long last, like Moses looking down at the land of milk and honey from Mount Sinai, Abdoulaye could see the 12 square kilometers of the promised land of Melilla spread out below him.

CHAPTER ELEVEN

ABDOULAYE'S ODYSSEY CONTINUES

Abdoulaye had made it to Mount Gourougou in Morocco near the border wall with Melilla. He found space in a tent with other migrants and listened with interest to the camp scuttlebutt to learn whatever might be useful to know.

There were asylum seekers from all over the world, as well as Africa, camped on the mountain. There were Syrians, Ukrainians, and a potpourri of other exiles, all fleeing the nightmarish situations in their native countries. Their white skins supposedly gave them access to preferential treatment at the border crossing.

It so happened that just when Abdoulaye arrived in June 2022, the encampment was in an uproar.

Two days before, hundreds of desperate migrants had swarmed the border walls at Melilla en masse. In the stampede, some had succeeded in making it through, but most had been turned back by the brutal border patrol tactics.

Both Moroccan and Spanish frontier police had turned their weapons on the people assaulting the wall. Border patrol officers were injured.

Thirty-three or thirty-seven fence climbers, the numbers varied, had been shot dead clinging to the wire mesh of the barriers. Most of the bodies had fallen 20 feet to the ground below. Those who had been snagged in the barbed wire were still being dismounted from their deadly perches. Scraps of tee shirts and lost shoes hung on the heights of the barricades like some kind of perverted decorations.

Abdoulaye heard all about the episode in the encampment, where most people could talk of nothing else. The Spanish press was up in arms that these atrocities could have happened. Public opinion on the Iberian peninsula was outraged on both sides of the issue. Both Spanish and Moroccan authorities pointed fingers at one another, denying that the bullets could have been fired by their nationals. Mainland Spaniards wanted to prove that no migrant had been killed on Spanish territory, as if that made any great difference to the horror which had occurred.

With feelings and tensions running so high, Abdoulaye thought that it might be wiser to wait to cross until things at the border had settled down to their normal slow boil. He was afraid to tempt fate despite his fake identity papers, Ekon Ibrahim's papers, which were supposedly his *passe-partout*, his *open sesame* to entrance through the wall.

Or was it just possible that all the upset and confusion might help him?

He heard via the migrant grapevine that the Moroccan authorities were planning to round up the refugees camped around Mount Gourougou and bus them back south as far as possible. In that case, Abdoulaye would almost be back to square one. He wasn't sure that he would have the heart to start all over again after such a setback.

He decided to risk going forward. He would rather fail while taking his chances moving ahead with Ekon Ibrahim's plan than fail due to an excess of caution or hesitation.

———

Losing no time, the young Senegalese presented himself at the border checkpoint the next morning. There was almost no one in line.

Two guards conferred over his papers and then took the documents into a little hut where a superior officer perused them carefully for what seemed like an hour.

Meanwhile, Abdoulaye was quaking in his threadbare shoes.

The border control officer made a quick phone call to someone. It took all Abdoulaye's self-control to stand there waiting, looking unconcerned.

After what seemed like an eternity, some underlings summoned him into the gatehouse.

The customs official stared at him fixedly from behind a metal desk upon which his *laissez-passer* document was lying. The man's gaze was moving back and forth from the document to Abdoulaye's face when he caught sight of the string bracelet.

"What's that on your wrist?" the officer asked Abdoulaye.

"It's my Ogoni amulet," the young man answered.

"You're free to go," said the Moroccan, who returned his documents to him, signaling to some soldiers who waved him out the door of the Customs hut and through the wire gate.

Another sheaf of papers was stuffed in his hand. These papers were from *Melilla Acoge,* a local organization that helped migrants overcome administrative, legal, and linguistic hurdles. They were instructions for where and how he could apply for asylum in Spain.

He had done it! He was in Europe! He couldn't stop himself from falling to his knees and resting his head on Spanish soil. It felt like any other sandy soil, but what a difference the ground on this side of the border made in terms of living standards, opportunity, and personal security!

————

Abdoulaye lost no time in applying for asylum at the Melilla Office of Asylum and Refuge, which was located right next to border control. He had heard that the two-week wait for approval could be much longer than that, even stretching years long for those from West Africa with very black skins like his own.

While waiting for certification, neither migrants nor asylum seekers had the right to work in Melilla. Luckily, there were volunteers on the ground at the CETI, Center for Temporary Lodging of Immigrants, who helped him out with food and shelter.

Abdoulaye's recent good luck held. Had repercussions from the deadly migrant incident at the fence helped him to get expedited treatment? It was said that the Spanish on the mainland were anxious to deflect negative world opinion, which condemned the shootings as unconscionable.

All Abdoulaye knew was his experience.

He waited out his two weeks at the migrant shelter in Melilla and was flown to Madrid to a migrant center in the Spanish capital city.

Ekon Ibrahim was taken there. Now, it was time to shed his false identity. Abdoulaye Diop rose like a phoenix from the ashes of his former assumed identity.

He was reborn in mainland Europe on the Iberian peninsula. Hallelujah! *Dieu soit merci!*

The next step was to find and throw himself on the mercy of Serigne M'Baye, the Spanish senator who was originally from Saint Louis, Sénégal, Abdoulaye's hometown.

With Serigne M'Baye's help, the young Senegalese was accepted into a work program for immigrants, which eventually led to legal EU residency if he dutifully fulfilled all the requirements for steady employment.

Abdoulaye spent some months working at the restaurant where he was assigned by his work program. There was a lot to learn about the organization of the kitchen, and the job was hard. He started at the bottom, doing the dirty tasks no one else wanted to do.

Abdoulaye happily accepted the conditions of his employment. After all, he was gainfully and legally employed. He had escaped the typical fate of most young Africans who debarked as clandestines in Madrid.

They had no choice but to join the organized bands of *manteros,* in other words, peddlers of counterfeit goods spread out on blankets, *mantas,* in all the main squares of the city, always running one step ahead of the police.

Through another busboy employed at his restaurant, Abdoulaye heard about a position working in the kitchen of the Dior Café near the ocean in Granville, France. Abdoulaye missed the ocean, and France was his ultimate goal. The fact that *Dior* reminded him of his own last name, *Diop,* seemed to augur well for the success of this move.

He jumped at the opportunity to work in Granville. Arrangements finalized, Abdoulaye called Alice on his new cell phone to come and meet him at Café Dior as soon as he got the new job duties there under his belt.

His responsibility for the safe delivery of the Ogoni oil deposit map weighed on him. The sooner he could transfer the document into Alice and Édouard's hands, the better.

CHAPTER TWELVE

AN EXCURSION TO NORMANDY

lthough enjoying the southwest of France, Sam and I
decided to make a little tour of Normandy before
flying home from Paris to Florida. Fall was in the
air. It was time for us to head back to Sarasota. Sam needed to
get back to his job, and we were both looking forward to seeing
our families in the United States. We hosted a farewell *apéro*
cocktail hour for our friends and acquaintances from
Montpezat and environs.

We arranged to store our Citroën *break* or station wagon
over the winter, parked in a big metal hangar with other cars
and *camping cars*, caravans, near the Caussade train station.
We disconnected the battery and crossed our fingers that the
car would restart nine months later when we returned to
France after the winter in Florida.

We picked up a rental car in Montauban, which we could
return at Charles de Gaulle airport after our ten-day circuit
around Normandy.

We were excited at the prospect of wandering around the
apple orchards, rich pasture lands, and scenic seacoast of the

old province of *les ducs de Normandie,* land of *le Calvados,* the famous apple brandy, oysters, and the memory of old-fashioned bathing machines.

We were looking forward to touring the famous beaches where the Allies had landed in WWII. We also wanted to see the Bayeux tapestry, which was conserved in the medieval town of that name. It depicted in stitchery how William, Duke of Normandy, had conquered England and become king in 1066.

Furthermore, our friends from Montpezat, Jean-Pierre and Claudie, had invited us to visit them at their house up north near Trouville and neighboring Deauville, names which made us think of the race track, casinos, and film festivals.

We agreed to rendezvous in Trouville-sur-Mer, a beach resort since the turn of the century. Jean-Pierre knew it well. He was going to show me how to time the tides, *les marées,* so I didn't have to walk over 500 meters of beach to put my toes in the water and go swimming.

———

Sam and I loved being on the road in the car, gabbing away together about everything and nothing as we rode along. There were companionable quiet times as well. We shared the driving.

We decided to break our journey to Normandy in Angoulême, a city about halfway on our route. We wouldn't be there at the right time to investigate, but Angoulême was known as the comic book capital of France for a festival that took place every January.

The French had a deep appreciation for comic books and cartoons, which they considered as the ninth art form after number eight, photography, and number seven, film. France had given a start in the 1950s to several world-famous cartoonists like Sempé and Goscinny. Sempé's elegant drawings were often about big city life. Eventually, during his long career, he drew many cartoons for the New Yorker, and his drawings were often featured on the prestigious magazine's cover.

Goscinny also ended up in the United States. He helped to create the beloved Astérix and Obélix series of books, illustrating the adventures of the heroes from ancient Gaul in Roman times: Astérix, a wiry little villager with a winged helmet, and his friend, Obélix, who was enormously strong and built like a boulder.

The festival started in Angoulême from modest beginnings in the 1970s when a few fanatical *BD* fans organized an exhibition of comic strip art. *BD*, pronounced *Bay Day,* is the French abbreviation of *bande dessinée,* which means comic strip. Over time, the exhibition turned into an international festival, which was now in its 50th iteration and had become identified with the little city. Paintings of famous cartoon characters like *Tintin,* created by Belgian cartoonist Hergé, decorated the walls of the old town along with *manga,* Japanese cartoons, and comics. All these and many others have become video creations that have expanded the purview of the festival.

Now that we had chosen Angoulême as a stopping point, Sam and I discussed where exactly to stay. There were city center hotels and lost in the countryside accommodations. There was a choice of modern, sleekly efficient places and old-fashioned, creaky, but charming inns.

We decided on an old inn, a former *relais de poste* where the horses that delivered the mail were changed over in olden times. The cost was a little over our usual budget, but the *relais* also featured a Michelin one-star restaurant where we could have dinner.

At the end of our four-hour drive, our rental car entered the courtyard of the inn through a narrow archway just as the old *diligences* pulled by horses had done.

The inn buildings were beautiful stonework. The *auberge* interior had handsome oak paneling, and the deep pile carpet muffled our steps as we followed the porter, *l'huissier*, who insisted on taking our bags.

We expected to be led to a comfortable but old-fashioned room with a pretty view over the rooftops of the city. The antique furniture would be complemented by *toile de Jouy* hangings softening the contours of the bed and the windows as vignettes of miniature lords and ladies disported themselves in a decorous eighteenth-century manner over and over and over again with the fabric repeat.

To our surprise, on the contrary, the interior of our room was the last word in modern, minimalist decor and conveniences. There was a giant flat-screen television on the soothing pale gray wall. The king-size bed still allowed plenty of space to move around the room. There were automatic controls for the window shades and drapes and for the many mood lighting options, which the porter demonstrated to us. The air conditioning was *le dernier cri*, the latest in efficiency and modulation. As soon as we were alone, we cranked it up and stretched out on the bed, basking in the welcome coolness.

"Ah," I said with a happy sigh, quoting as best as I could remember a snatch of Baudelaire which popped into my mind, "*Ici, tout est luxe, calme et volupté.*" Richness, quietness, and pleasure.

Sam turned his head on the pillow and smiled at me. "I love our little *escapades*, Barbara, a little romantic getaway, just the two of us. A final adventure before we return home to Florida and I go back to work."

We smiled at one another in complicity.

After a rest, we sampled the delights of the state-of-the-art plumbing in the shower and bath, water shooting out from many angles at adjustable pressures and temperatures. Even the hair dryer in the bathroom was especially powerful, and I felt my blow dry came out better than usual. We went down to dinner refreshed and in good spirits.

Seated in the pretty garden of the hotel, where meals were served in nice weather, we studied the tempting menu. We both decided on the *menu fraîcheur,* which seemed well-suited to the warm evening. It was *tataki de saumon,* salmon tartare, *médaillon de lieu jaune,* Dover hake with champagne sauce, dal of lentils and crunchy vegetables and for dessert, a pistachio macaron creation with fresh raspberries. Each course was arranged on its plate with care in an artistic way. A pleasure for the eyes as well as the palate.

There was no rush. We had become accustomed to the unhurried pace in French restaurants, where fast service was not as appreciated as in the United States. Instead, the hallmark of fine dining was to be leisurely. Taking time between the apéritif and ordering the meal was part of the ritual. The same held true for a pause for conversation and anticipation to build between each course while it was prepared. Coffee, if desired, came after the dessert, which prolonged the time spent at the table. Diners were expected to ask for the check when they were ready instead of being automatically presented with the bill at the end of their meal. A fine meal was a sensual experience and the evening's entertainment all in one.

The next morning, after breakfast in the lovely garden of the old inn, Sam and I drove north and crossed over into Normandy.

Normandy is divided into five *départements*: Calvados with the cities of Bayeux and Caen, Manche with the city of Cherbourg, Seine-Maritime with Rouen and the port of Le Havre. Orne's big city was Alençon of lace fame, and Eure was closest to Paris with Giverny and Évreux, where JP had a house.

We were supposed to meet up with our friends from Montpezat in Trouville on the beach. However, JP and Claudie had a change of heart.

They called and instructed us to rendezvous with them instead at Monet's house in Giverny. We could visit the gardens and then have a late lunch together at *la Maison Baudy,* where they had reserved a table.

"Sounds like a plan," Sam told them on the phone. "Barbara and I will try to get an early start and meet up with you on time."

"We'll be waiting at the museum entrance with the tickets," Claudie said. "*À toute,*" which was short for *à tout à l'heure,* see you in a bit.

It turned out to be fun to meet up with our Montpezat friends in Giverny. We had a wonderful visit to Monet's house. We admired the way the artist had painted the rooms in different bright colors and the contrasting moldings, too.

The garden was a riot of colorful blooms. We followed the

path around to the lily pond he had created a short stroll away from the house. After many photo ops posing for each other on the Japanese-style bridge over the pond, we ended up back in the *atelier* and gift shop, which had a big photo of Claude Monet in old age wearing a suit, his brushes in his hand, still at work painting.

Our lunch reservation was just down Giverny's one street at *Maison Baudy*, which had been serving food to village visitors since the Impressionists' time. In fact, many of the painters themselves had enjoyed a former Madame Baudy's hospitality. Renoir, Rodin, Sisley and Pisarro, and Monet himself, among others, had eaten there.

L'Hôtel Baudy, attached to the restaurant, was sometimes known as the American painters' hotel because it had sheltered John Singer Sargent, Theodore Robinson, Mary Cassatt, Theodore Butler, who married into Monet's family, and a host of American impressionist artists.

They had come to paint the beauty of the banks of the Seine and stayed to be inspired by the presence of the master, Claude Monet.

"It's so nice here on this restaurant terrace," Barbara said as we sat down at our table. "How did you ever find this place?"

"Oh, we've been coming here for years," Claudie said. "Right, JP? You knew about it first, didn't you?"

JP is pronounced *Jee-Pay* in French since the letter J is *Jee* and G is *Jay*. It had taken me a while to learn to make this reversal in my mind, and it still didn't feel natural.

Jean-Pierre responded, "Well, yes. My house in Évreux is only thirty minutes away. I've known about it forever. After lunch, I want to show Sam and Barbara the restaurant's garden across the road. That is where the American Impressionist painters painted in a little hut, *la cabanne*, which is still there."

"But first, let's order. The food is good. I recommend the menu at 30 euros. They have *saumon sauce normande* today. I love that creamy *veloutée sauce*. I think I'll order a bottle of *le Morgon* for us. What do you think, Sam?"

Sam replied, "Yes, I prefer red wine. *Le Morgon* goes with everything. It seems like a great choice to me."

After ordering four menus of the day, I asked Claudie a question that had been on my mind.

"Claudie," I inquired, "Do you know anything about an ex-governor of Nigeria, retired in or near Montpezat? *Très British*."

"Hmm," Claudie said thoughtfully. "*Non, désolée*. I don't think so. Hicham Nchini lives in Montpezat. He's Moroccan and definitely not *très British*. The only other African person I can think of in Montpezat is the black man with the white skull cap who used to walk in the *rue de la Libération* sometimes. That's your old street, Barbara and Sam."

I rummaged around in my memory. A light bulb went on. "Right," I said. "I know who you mean. There was a little guy who walked from the top of the street to *la place* around lunchtime. I wonder what happened to him. I haven't seen him in some time. He had very dark skin and dressed like a devout Muslim with his crocheted cap and loose-fitting white clothes. He was so quiet and unobtrusive, but even so, he stuck out. Who was he? Where was he going at lunchtime? Everything is closed at that hour."

"Well, it's very interesting," Claudie replied. "I've heard that the gentleman was the subaltern of an English army officer who brought him back to France from his African campaigns. The two old men preferred not to be separated when the Colonel retired. They had spent their lives together as officer and orderly in Africa, so it suited both of them to keep up the same arrangement back in France."

"Hah, that's kind of a Victorian story," said Sam, who had been listening.

"Well, I'm not sure that it is accurate," Claudie said, "but that's the rumor."

The wine came and was approved and poured out. We toasted one another. *"Santé! Chin, chin!* Good health to us! Cheers!"

Barbara complimented JP. "You certainly know your wines, Jean-Pierre. I love it when you make the selection. I get to taste something interesting every time. Where did you learn how to do that?"

JP laughed with pleasure. "I think it's just being born a Frenchman, Barbara. No special skill or study required."

"Were you born in Évreux or nearby? I know you're very proud of your *normand* background."

"No, no," JP told us. "As Claudie already knows, I was born and grew up in another part of Normandy from here. I was raised in Granville in *Manche. La Manche* is how you say the English Channel in French. Of course, we don't call it the 'English' Channel. In French, it's always been called the sleeve because of its shape."

"Hah, that's cute." We all chuckled.

"I wish you and Sam could visit Granville, Barbara," Jean-Pierre said. "I'm very fond of it there. The houses have a lot of British influence. I'd love for you to see it."

"Well, we're as free as birds for ten days until our flight home. Maybe we could put it on the itinerary," Sam suggested to me.

"Why not?" I said. *"Je suis partante.* I like that idea. Someplace a little different."

CHAPTER THIRTEEN

THE DIOR MUSEUM

Sam and I stayed with Claudie and JP at the beach for a few days before heading west to Granville.

It was quite different from Trouville-sur-Mer, which had been a seaside resort since the turn of the century.

Granville, on the other hand, was a deep port. We arrived and parked near the harbor of the dark, blue ocean.

It was lunchtime. We ate in a cute restaurant right by the docks. It was crowded. It was August in France, and many people were on vacation. The cuisine was good and inventive, and I ordered my new favorite oysters called 'Utah.'

At the fish market in Trouville, I tasted a certain variety of oysters for the first time. They were found on Utah Beach, one of the big Allied landing beaches. They grew very large and were highly esteemed for their distinctive, nutty flavor. I didn't know what their name had been before the Americans called the beach Utah, but that was their name now, *les huitres utah.*

During lunch, we discovered that Christian Dior's childhood home was located not far from the town proper and open to visitors. We decided to go there and check it out.

The beautiful villa high above the town was now a museum dedicated to the memory of the famous couturier who brought French fashion back to life after WWII with his 'new look.'

The house was a charming seaside villa painted pink with white gingerbread trim. It reminded me a bit of the turn of the century 'cottages' in Newport, Rhode Island. Dior's parents must have been very affluent.

The house was set in a lovely rose garden where refreshments were served in a little cafe for visitors. The property overlooked some beautiful, wild beaches far below the promontory where it sat. Parasailers and paragliders swept along, high in the French blue sky, as we looked out at the stupendous view over the tall trees and wild greenery on the cliff that descended down to the Atlantic Ocean.

I read there was a path down to the beach that the Diors had used, but I couldn't see where it began.

It turned out that Sam wasn't interested in visiting the house. He preferred to relax over a cup of coffee in the garden restaurant.

I wanted to go inside the museum, so we arranged to meet afterward in the refreshment area. I got a ticket and waited in line at the entrance to the house.

I was surprised to read that the theme of the present show was Dior's African collections from summer 2021 and Cruise Wear 2020. I didn't realize that Dior had been influenced by Africa.

When I got inside, I saw that the integrity of the house had been preserved. Visitors could see the dining room, conservatory, library, and upstairs bedrooms. The restrained decoration of the moldings and marble floors made a contrast with Monet's much more individualistic and homey house, which we had visited in Giverny. *Chez Dior*, the walls and trim were not painted bright blue and yellow like *chez Monet*. Instead, the Dior villa was decorated in exquisite neutral colors of impeccable taste.

The Dior house had now been arranged with museum showcases holding mannequins dressed in a riot of African lost wax fabrics. The material was sewn into elegant and creative garments of rich complexity and meticulous craftsmanship, accessorized with intricate beadwork and stitching.

Shoes, hats, and jewelry had been created to complement each outfit using straw, feathers, crystals, and flowers. The designers' imagination had been given free rein and then made into wearable clothing by the expertise of the seamstresses and tailors, *les petites mains*.

I read on an information card that the Ghanaian artist Amoako Boafo, who was a new darling of the international art world, had collaborated on the 2021 collection. His portraits and paintings had been adapted to decorate the tee shirts, trousers, and other clothing.

I saw clothes from the Dior 2020 cruise collection, which was first shown at the El Badi Palace in Morocco. Marrakech in Morocco was where Christian Dior's first successor, Yves Saint Laurent, had a house, so there was a longtime Moroccan connection with the Dior fashion house.

Famous couturier Pathe O from Burkina Faso, known for making some of Nelson Mandela's shirts, was another collaborator from his *atelier* in Ivory Coast.

I took a bunch of photos of the exhibits to show Sam, amusing myself, carefully reading the descriptive placards by the showcases. For an hour, I wandered around, totally immersed in this fantasy world of fashion. Then I remembered that Sam was waiting for me outside.

When I joined him at his table in the garden, he was not alone. He was sitting with a handsome, young, black woman. I was taken aback for a moment. Then I realized he was with Alice Blancpain, from *La Table d'Alice* restaurant in Caussade. At first, I hadn't recognized her out of context.

I said, "Sam, look who you've found! *Bonjour, Alice.* What a nice surprise!"

"*Bonjour, Madame.* Yes, your husband here recognized me and kindly invited me to have a coffee with him."

Alice was polite but seemed as surprised to see us as we were to see her.

People from *le Tarn-et-Garonne* did not usually get around much. A trip of 125 kilometers to Dordogne or Corrèze was considered very far by the standards of the *Causscadais* or the *Montpezatais*. Here was Alice, 800 kilometers away from home. I wondered who was watching little Manu. It seemed odd that his devoted mother would feel enough at ease to leave him after the attempted abduction just a month ago.

"How did you like the Dior exhibition?" Alice asked me.

"I loved the whole visit," I replied. "What a nice lifestyle the Dior family must have led in this beautiful setting. I also enjoyed seeing the African-inspired couture. I had no idea that the house of Dior had created African collections."

"Yes, it was groundbreaking recognition for African fashion, which continues to develop an international reputation. It set my native country and the whole continent on fire with excitement to be appreciated by the house of Dior for our sense of design and craft expertise. I made a special trip here to Normandy to see the clothes and materials that some of my countrymen fabricated using traditional craftsmanship," Alice explained. Just then, Alice stood up, and I noticed her dress. It was a soft golden color covered in an elegant lost wax print like the ones in the exhibit.

"Please excuse me," she said. "Thank you for the drink and the conversation, but I must be on my way."

This was a bit unexpected. The young woman seemed anxious to be rid of us. *Was she meeting someone here?*

At that very moment, the soft music that had been playing in the background of the refreshment area changed to a loud, toe-tapping number. Everybody sitting on the lawn chairs and at the tables perked up and looked around for the source of the music. It seemed to be coming from the food preparation hut.

Alice looked as surprised as the rest of us.

A handsome, young African man also emerged from the hut. He danced across the lawn in time with the music, smiling and sashaying as he went. He headed right for Alice, wearing her distinctive Senegalese designer wear, took her in his arms, and started whirling her around in time with the music. They made a lovely couple moving in synchrony to the joyous music. They looked so happy together. They seemed to know one another.

Was this entertainment planned?

After a bit, a second couple joined them on the grass, and then another. One song ended, and another began. Several more couples took the floor, I mean the grass.

The dancing was just really getting going when two uniformed officials started walking across the expansive lawn toward us. Their grim faces looked very out of place in this setting. *Were they going to put a stop to the dancing?*

Alice's dance partner deftly danced away from her, gave a little bow, and ran off full speed on graceful cat's feet toward the edge of the garden. A paraglider was sitting there idle. He quickly strapped himself into the contraption. Then he sat down in the pillowy, hammock-like seat and pushed himself off the edge of the cliff into the air with his feet.

For a moment, the paraglider fell into the void, but then it was swept aloft with a fair breeze. The pilot zigzagged back and forth on the air currents to gain altitude. Soon, he was high above our upturned heads, headed out over the ocean.

The crowd was transfixed by the air acrobatics. *Was this some kind of performance? Was it part of the entertainment?*

People started to clap in admiration for the daring stunt. Sam and I were oohing and aahing, clapping along with everyone else.

Not Alice, however. Alice started to cry softly to herself, a wary eye on the beefy security officers who had run to the edge of the cliff after the paraglider.

"Alice, can we help you? Please tell us what we can do?" I said, genuinely moved by her distress.

Sam asked her, "Do you have a car parked up here? May we take you to your hotel? Where are you staying?"

Alice let herself be led away from the garden, and we steered her toward our car, which was parked on a residential street a short distance from the Dior mansion. She was distraught. She kept murmuring something. It was hard to make out exactly what she was saying, but it sounded like a name.

We helped her into our car, and we all sat down. The box of tissues from the dashboard came in handy. When Alice had cried herself out somewhat, she choked out the reason for her distress in a quavering voice:

"That man I was dancing with, he was my half-brother, Abdoulaye. He came all the way from Africa. We were to meet at the Dior Museum restaurant. He let me know he was working in the kitchen there. I haven't seen him in so long. We were going to be reunited after years of separation. Our families were estranged. But now he's run off again. How did he know how to fly that paraglider? It's dangerous! Where has he gone? I've lost him again."

Sam and I looked at one another incredulously.

Alice continued with her lament. "Where will he be able to land? He made it all the way to France over the ocean from Senegal, and now he may crash into the sea and drown anyway!"

Her slim shoulders started to tremble, and she burst out in another bout of tears.

What could Sam or I say? We were totally out of our depth. We didn't really know Alice, and she didn't even really know us. We were just customers from the restaurant back in Caussade.

"Abdoulaye, *mon petit frère*," Alice sobbed again, intoning her half-brother's name over and over like a prayer.

The poor young woman, who had always seemed so self-possessed, was entirely undone by this predicament. She was involved in some private nightmare which was none of our business.

As Sam and I looked at one another, puzzled how to proceed, we were all startled by an imperative rapping on the driver's side window.

To our astonishment, François Lamy, the dealer in African arts from the *Africajarc* festival, was knocking imperiously on the car window. Through the glass, he glowered at us and commanded Sam to roll down the window. He raised his fist, reminding me of the 'power figure' African statuette, and shouted that he wanted to talk to Alice. His manner was very threatening.

Sam made a lightning decision. He put the car in gear, and we drove off down the street, leaving Monsieur Lamy behind us on the pavement, shaking his fist, looking angry and exasperated.

Behind him, approaching at a fast trot, we saw the uniformed men from the restaurant coming to meet him. Their uniforms said *DOUANES FRANÇAISES. Were they really Customs and Border police or some kind of armed guards?*

CHAPTER FOURTEEN

CHASING THE PARAGLIDER

S am drove the Citroën down the steep hill back toward Granville harbor with me sitting in the passenger seat beside him and Alice sitting in the back of the car behind us. We were all shaken up by the sudden, threatening appearance of the Africana art dealer from the *Tarn-et-Garonne.* It was a relief to be putting some distance between us and him.

I asked Sam if he had seen those border patrol policemen hurrying toward Monsieur Lamy. Sam nodded his head and said quietly that he had spotted them.

"Alice," I asked, "what is Monsieur Lamy doing here? Why was he shouting and glowering at us? Were those *douaniers,* customs agents, with him? Were they the reason that your half-brother ran off like that?"

Alice, who had just somewhat calmed down from her distress over the paraglider, started to despair again, repeating, "I don't know. I don't know. *Je ne sais pas.*"

Sam said to me, "Hmmm. It doesn't look like we're going to learn very much from Madame Alice right now. Where shall we take her? And in her present upset condition."

I was working up to asking Alice where we should take her when she tapped me on the shoulder from the back seat with her long, elegant fingers. "*Regardez! C'est un parapente!* Look, it's a paraglider," she said as she pointed urgently to the sky ahead of us, her eyes riveted upwards.

Sam shielded his eyes with his hand to see better, and I craned my neck to look up in the sky. *Yep. There was a paraglider up ahead of us, flying high in the sky. Was it Alice's brother? It could be, I supposed.*

Once again, Sam made a command decision. He said, "Let's follow it as long as we can, *Mesdames*. Maybe we'll get lucky enough to keep it in sight until it lands."

And so we followed the paraglider's path north along the coast of Normandy's *département de la Manche*. We left Granville behind. A sign said we were on the *Cotentin* peninsula. After 20 kilometers or so, we passed *Briqueville sur Mer*, a little beach resort completely rebuilt after WWII. The roads got smaller and became two lanes. No more *départmental* highways. We got to an impasse around Bréhal, which was not on the sea but inland where the trees blocked our view of the paraglider, and we thought we had lost it.

"This is like one of those car rallies I used to read about in *Road and Track*, where a driving club met on Sunday morning to follow a course with clues to find a treasure. I always wanted to do that," I told Sam and Alice.

Alice was totally focused on spotting the paraglider again, but Sam responded, "Well, you're getting to have a rally experience now, Barbara. I have to admit it's kind of fun for me driving as fast as I can legally go, trying to follow the will o' the wisp up there in the sky. I feel like Mario Andretti."

"Yeah," I said to Sam. "It's like a slalom course for us too. *N'est-ce pas, Alice?* Right, Alice?"

Alice had considerably perked up now that we were on the move. She nodded in agreement with me and showed how she was holding on to the grab handle above the back door as the car went around the bends in the road.

I tried to bolster her more positive mood as well as my own. "I think we're going to find your paraglider, Alice," I said. "And Sam, you are doing a great job at the wheel. But now, where do we go?"

We were stopped at the crossing of two little roads. The signs said *Haut Menil* to the right and *Bas Menil* to the left. You could choose between going to the hamlets of High Menil or Low Menil. We were really nowhere, the boondocks, *le trou du monde*. By the side of the road, I noticed a monument with an American flag on it. I read the English translation of the French inscription aloud:

USA

In memory of the lieutenant Charles E. Stone, American aviator, 109th Tactical Squadron of the

9th US Army AirForce, shot down on the 6th of June 1944 at Menil about 5:20 pm - and

American soldiers, shot down the 30th of July 1944, Arthur D. Muthig, Berlin A. Fenton and

Robert W. Grow, 6th Armored Division of General George S. Patton's 3rd Army.

SHOT DOWN GLORIOUSLY FOR THE BRÉHAL LIBÉRATION

- REMEMBER -

- SOUVENEZ-VOUS -

Even a ways inland from the beaches, many Allied soldiers were lost in the days after the DDay landings. No wonder the memory of all the young lives sacrificed to free France was still very much alive in Normandy.

We were somber for a moment when Alice started to bounce up and down in her seat with excitement. "*Regardez, regardez. Le voilà, tout droit au-dessus de ces arbres!* Look, look!" she said. "I see the paraglider ahead above those trees."

And indeed, there it was again.

Sam pressed on the accelerator, and we raced off down the little country road. After many twists and turns, we were back on a bigger highway heading toward *Avranches,* according to the signpost. We were going south now, not north any longer.

The paraglider had done an about-face. It was easier to follow over the increasingly low, marshy landscape. As our car navigated the way through the crooked streets of a little village, we whizzed by a café, a restaurant, another fancier restaurant, and the church. We passed the town hall, which said *Genêts* above the entrance, and a row of houses with blue hydrangeas, *des hortensias,* blooming by the doorways.

To our right, away in the distance, one of the most famous silhouettes in France appeared. It was *le Mont Saint Michel,* the beautiful island abbey founded in the sixth century and crowned by a church in the 12th century. It had attracted pilgrims from time immemorial. Le Mont Saint Michel was the second most visited sight in France after Paris.

The gothic spire of the hilltop church created a delicate, fairy-like tracery against the sky from this distance. And to think that the tides used to cut the island off from land once a day or more! That was great protection against attackers in medieval times. Now, the tourist invaders could walk over the new footbridge from the car park anytime.

We admired the iconic view of the abbey as we rocketed along, following the paraglider's path in the air from below on land as best we could. The church was framed against the sky on its little islet out in the *la baie du Mont Saint Michel.* The bay led out to the Atlantic Ocean.

Sam brought the car to an abrupt stop. The paraglider was no longer to be seen. We sat there scanning the heavens for a while, waiting for it to reappear. Nothing. We were stymied.

"*Ah, non,*" Alice sighed, disgusted. " *Il n'y est plus.* We've lost him." Her voice skipped a beat, "If it was ever him at all."

CHAPTER FIFTEEN

MAN DOWN

T he big, wide expanse of sky over *le Mont Saint Michel* and its bay was now empty except for a few low clouds. Sam had pulled the car onto the side of the road. He, Alice, and I got very quiet. We didn't see the parachute-like apparatus up in the sky anymore.

We noticed a little sign by the road that pointed the way to *le camping St Michel*. We nodded to one another, and Sam made a hard right turn onto the little track. The sides of the dirt road were covered with scrubby little trees and bushes, leaving just enough room for two cars to pass. After about 750 *mètres*, the road seemed to lead nowhere. We were about to turn back when the bushes parted, and we saw the campground.

It was full of people milling about, relaxing in front of their tents and caravans. Many small *camping cars* were parked in neat rows on the space cleared in front of a big expanse of sand and scrub ground from which we had a good view of *le Mont Saint Michel* shimmering in the distance.

At one end of the big clearing, there was an information center and a ramshackle snack bar. Everyone seemed to be in a holiday mood. *What was going on here?*

I put my window down and said to a group lounging on beach chairs in front of their camper, *"Bonjour messieurs-dames. Qu'est-ce que c'est ici? Un camping?* What is this place? A campground?"

One young man stood up and detached himself from his family group. He came over to the car to explain. *"Oui, c'est un camping, mais avec une petite différence.* We're camping all right, but the difference is that we are either on our way to or coming back from *le Mont Saint Michel.* You see it over there. It's 7 kilometers away, about an hour's walk."

Sam said, "You can walk to *le Mont Saint Michel* from here? *C'est génial!* That's great! Barbara, maybe we could do that, too."

The young man continued, "We are waiting for our guide to cross the sands. We made a reservation for our group quite a while ago. We're going tomorrow. We've been planning this pilgrimage for a long time."

"Oh, I see," Sam said. "You need a reservation."

"Yes, the walk isn't difficult, but it is dangerous to cross without a guide to lead you away from the areas of quicksand and unstable ground, which vary due to the tides. Do you see those poles out there?"

We all looked out toward the island. "No," I said, "I don't see anything."

"Well, perhaps it's hard to see from here, but there are some poles with raised platforms along the way to the Mount. In case walkers are taken by surprise by the incoming tide, they can climb up above the water and wait for rescue."

"He seems to know a lot about this. *Il est bien informé*," Alice said to Sam and me.

Overhearing her, our informant agreed. "Yes, I know all about the walk. We do it almost every year. You can make arrangements at the office over there," he said, gesturing toward the building near the snack bar. "But at this time in the summer, there's about a two-week wait for a guided trip. *Bonne chance.* Good luck."

I thought, *What a good idea, to walk to le Mont Saint Michel on foot! Just like the pilgrims in the Middle Ages! That way you could avoid the foot traffic jam and the big car park. You could arrive at the island in all serenity, 'en toute sérénité,' and start the climb up the hill to the beautiful church.*

I said aloud to Alice and Sam, "I visited *le Mont Saint Michel* once a long time ago. I remember climbing up the steep street lined with boutiques and souvenir shops to the church.

First, I ate *une omelette* at the restaurant *la Mère Poularde.* It was cooked over the open fireplace according to her famous omelet recipe. We also ate *belons,* big oysters from the Bay of Mont St. Michel and *l'agneau pré-salé.*"

"*L'agneau pré-salé?* What's that?" Sam wanted to know.

Alice, ever the restaurateur, answered him. "It's lamb that has been raised on the meadows near the sea around here. At high tide, the land where the animals graze is submerged. The salty taste of the grass they eat at low tide subtly influences the taste of the lamb. It's called *l'agneau pré-salé,* salty prairie lamb. *C'est délicieux.*"

I said to Alice, "Yes, I remember that too. It was delicious."

Then, turning to Sam, I said, "Walking to the mount sounds like a great excursion, but a two-week waiting list? It's not in the cards for us this year anyway, Sam. We have our flight home to Florida in a couple of days."

"Alice," I said, turning to face her lovely visage over the back of the front seat, "what shall we do? Where would you like us to take you? We seem to have lost sight of the paraglider. Do you have the train schedule back to Caussade from Normandy?"

Alice considered a moment. When she spoke, she was quite decisive. "Thank you for all you have done. *Merci mille fois pour tout ce que vous avez fait.* I think it best that I stay on nearby here for a few days. I might pick up the trail of my half-brother. I need to find out if he is alright. If you could take me to that little hotel we passed on the main road, I think I'll stay there for tonight. I've got my *brosse à dents* in my *trousse* here," she said, indicating her fashionably oversized purse, which could easily hold a toothbrush and other overnight necessities.

"Édouard will want to know how I'm doing, of course, and I want to check on little Manu. I'll call the restaurant and let them know my plans."

"Why don't we take you to the police station?" I suggested. "Surely it's time to involve the authorities. They could help."

"*Non!*" Alice replied definitively. Something steely in her manner told me to back off.

From the other side of the campground, we suddenly heard shouting. "*Hé! Ho!*"

A crowd of people had gathered and was calling and waving their arms over their heads to someone out on the sand to get his attention. "*Attention! C'est dangereux!* It's dangerous!" they cried.

Sam immediately turned the wheel and headed over to see what was happening. Once parked, we jumped out of the car and hurried toward the tidal flats, where everyone was staring intently at a figure on the horizon. "*Vous permettez?*" Alice asked a bystander holding binoculars.

The man nodded and handed her the field glasses. Grabbing them, she peered through, adjusting the lenses for her eyes.

I watched with concern as she fell to her knees on the sand and began shouting. "It's Abdoulaye! *C'est lui, mon frère,* Abdoulaye! *Dieu soit merci!* Thank God! He's safe!" Her body relaxed as she handed us the binoculars to have a look for ourselves.

Sam and I were jubilant, along with Alice, when we, too, had our turn at the glasses. We saw the small figure of a young African man in a white tee shirt and jeans out in the distance.

Everyone, including ourselves, was waving and shouting at him. Some people were trying to warn him to be careful.

Just then, a figure of evident authority set off from the beach toward Abdoulaye.

The man with the binoculars told us, "*C'est Alain.* He's one of the guides. He'll help your friend to walk safely to the shore. Lucky for him that Alain hadn't left for the day."

Twenty minutes later, Abdoulaye was safely on the beach of the campground. He and Alain were surrounded by well-wishers. People were clapping them on the back.

Abdoulaye had a huge smile on his face when he spied Alice. He looked bedraggled but happy.

People were offering the returnees bottles of water and cans of beer. Everyone was celebrating.

"What were you doing out there, *jeune homme?*" an older man with tattoos and a gray ponytail asked Abdoulaye. "*Tu es fou?*" he wanted to know. "Don't you know it's crazy to be out there with the evening tide coming in? It can rise 46 feet or *14 mètres* in a few hours."

"He got separated from his group," someone suggested.

"He had a big date this evening, and he couldn't wait until tomorrow to get off the island," another person said, pointing at lovely Alice. Everybody laughed.

Abdoulaye laughed, too. He put one arm around Alice's waist and took another big swig from a water bottle. Then, he motioned for the crowd to be quiet. He explained to us:

"I was paragliding a little ways north of here when I got caught in an updraft." He winked at Alice to show he knew he was leaving out just where and how he got the paraglider.

"It took me a while to learn to maneuver the paraglider. It was my first attempt at paragliding, and the air currents were steady, thank goodness, but *capricieux,* capricious.

When I finally got turned around again, heading south, I overshot my mark. I saw the big sand flats around that island with the church on it, but I was afraid to bail out over land. So I went down in the water. I was just congratulating myself on my successful landing when the paraglider started being pulled out to sea by the wind. Whew! *Ouf!* Let me tell you, I had some time trying to get myself unattached from the parachute. The wind caught it like a sail. But I did it!

My next problem was how to get back to shore. Luckily, where I grew up in Senegal, I learned to swim almost before I could walk. The ocean holds no terrors for me. And the incoming tide was in my favor. So here I am, *sain et sauf,* safe and sound. Thanks to a little extra help from Alain here." Abdoulaye flashed Alain a big smile.

One thing led to another, and soon, pretty much the whole campground was involved in *apéro* hour. We shared plastic cups of wine with the pilgrims. Alain was toasted. "*Santé!*" "*À la votre!*" "*À la tienne!* To everybody's good health!"

Potato chips, rounds of sausage, and little cubes of cheese appeared. We all helped ourselves.

We met people from the Netherlands and Germany, as well as men and women from all over France.

A man from Belgium told Abdoulaye how lucky he had been to catch on to how to steer the paraglider on his first flight. "Paragliding isn't so easy. I know. I've done it. You are a very quick learner, and the winds were with you. I think you should buy a lottery ticket today." They both laughed.

After an hour or so, it became clear that Abdoulaye was fading. He was exhausted after his mid-air exploits and subsequent dunking in the ocean. We said our *bonsoirs* and *mercis* all around to the assembled group and took our leave.

We got in the car and headed back to the village, where Alice remembered passing a little hotel. Luckily, it wasn't *complet* that night, and they had rooms for our tired selves.

Happily worn out from our eventful day, warmed by the wine and hunger appeased by the *apéro* snacks, we all retired for the night without even a thought of dinner. But not before we overheard Alice and Abdoulaye whispering conspiratorially together.

"*Tu l'as toujours, mon frère? Tu ne l'as pas perdu?*" Alice hissed a bit frenziedly at Abdoulaye, as if afraid of his reply. "Do you still have the map of the oil deposit?" she asked him.

"*Sois cool, ma petite Alice. À l'aise, ma petite soeur. Aucun problème,*" her half-brother answered, his white teeth shining in a triumphant smile as he told her there was no problem.

He had not lost the map. He had it with him. It was safe and sound.

CHAPTER SIXTEEN

FLORIDA BOUND

S am and I drove Alice and Abdoulaye to the train station in Le Havre. From there, they were headed back to Caussade to reunite the map of the oil deposit with the N'kisi Kongo statue and Alice with Edouard and little Manu. Abdoulaye had a job waiting for him with them at *La Table d'Alice,* which would qualify as part of his program to earn French residency. In five years, if his employment record was consistent and he had otherwise an unblemished record, he could apply for full European Union citizenship.

As we were waiting for the train to arrive, Alice and Abdoulaye wanted to thank us for our help. They took us into their confidence and explained to us all about the oil deposit map from Africa and the corresponding N'Kisi Kongo figure waiting back in Caussade. Their pleasure and excitement at the prospect of putting together the two halves of the oil deposit puzzle together was contagious.

Sam and I exchanged knowing looks. We finally understood the reason for the phony N'Kisi Kongo carving, which had caused François Lamy to act so strangely. It had been fabricated for a special purpose.

Alice and her younger half-brother told us about the plight of the Ogoni tribe down south in Nigeria. It sounded as if this oil discovery would benefit a worthy cause once Édouard got things in motion.

As thanks for our help, Alice promised us a special meal on the house at *La Table d'Alice* when we returned to the *Tarn-et-Garonne* early next summer. We said goodbye, and they boarded the train.

———

Sam and I spent the rest of the day in Le Havre, an important cross-Channel ferry port and the largest container port in France. The city had been basically flattened by Allied bombing during the war and rebuilt in a blocky, utilitarian style afterward.

Le Havre represented a memory for me. I had docked here on my second visit to France in 1968 as a passenger on the ship *France,* the pride of the French ocean liners.

It was the start of my junior year in college, and I was studying for a year at the Sorbonne in Paris and receiving college credit through an accredited American junior year abroad program. There was a group of about 25 of us traveling from America. We disembarked in the evening, and after a night at a little hotel, we took an early morning train south to Biarritz on the Bay of Biscay to take a six-week French immersion course before heading to Paris to attend the Sorbonne. I hardly got to see Le Havre then, so I was excited that Sam and I had some time to poke around.

Our first stop was the Le Havre City Museum, which looked out on the enormous expanse of the waters of the English Channel, *la Manche,* as it was called in French. The museum had a fine collection of small paintings by the artist Eugene Boudin. Boudin specialized in painting scenes of the nearby beaches at Trouville, Deauville, and Honfleur, where 19th-century ladies with parasols and gentlemen in top hats strolled or picnicked on the sand. The painter had the gift of capturing the incredible cloud formations and changing skies over the Atlantic. His canvases were small gems which influenced the Impressionists.

———

Rather than spend our last night in France in Le Havre, we decided to top off our visit to Normandy with a night in Étretat. We wanted to see the famous cliff formation while we were in the vicinity. We could return our rental car to the Paris CDG airport the next day in time for our flight back to the United States.

Driving toward Étretat, we saw road signs for Calais. I had read that the big migrant camps right near the Channel Tunnel entrance that had caused so much dissension between the French and the English had, for all intents and purposes, been broken up.

For many years, migrants seeking a way across the Channel had congregated near Calais, hoping to smuggle themselves aboard one of the many trucks headed for England from the European Continent. They attempted to secret themselves in containers or hid between boxes of merchandise or under piles of produce. Some migrants even made it across the channel hidden in the wheel wells of big semi-trailers for the thirty-five-minute ride to the English side.

"You know, Sam," I said, "I read recently that with the new technology applied to cross-Channel traffic, illegal migration from Calais to Dover has effectively ended. Even the largest trucks are x-rayed now, and there is no longer a way for a person to hide anymore."

"Very interesting," Sam said, adding that he had heard about another effective deterrent to stowaways.

He had read that trucks now had to wait out an obligatory two-week quarantine period on the French side of the channel before they started the trip to England. This extra time added to the trip made it almost impossible to stay hidden aboard long enough to arrive alive at the other end.

"What do you think about this migration crisis? Take Abdoulaye's example, and he was so fortunate."

I shook my head in mystification and frustration. "I just don't know where or when it will end. We may be talking about resettling a huge portion of the world's population."

We were both quiet, contemplating the unthinkable disruptions a program of that nature would involve. Sometimes, it was an advantage to be our age and know that other younger people with new ideas would have to work out the solutions to the many problems facing our planet.

"It's too much for me," I admitted to Sam. "I prefer to concentrate on the happy outcome for Abdoulaye in which we played a tiny role."

"Yes," Sam continued along my thought lines. "Maybe this treasure map he's taking to Édouard will improve the lives of disadvantaged Ogoni tribesmen down there in the Niger Delta so they can live decently on their ancestral lands. We had some small part in the effort to make that happen, even if it was only by chance."

———

Ten minutes later, we arrived in Étretat. There was a line of cars on the Main Street, *la rue principale*. It looked like it was not going to be easy to find a parking place in such a busy tourist town.

Like the other visitors, we had come to see the town's picturesque stone arch and needle formation sticking out in the ocean. At the moment, it was nowhere in sight.

Sam said, "I see a lot of traffic, Barbara, but I don't see the cliff. It's familiar to me from Monet's paintings. It was one of his favorite subjects."

I replied, "Let's get settled at the hotel first, and then we can look for the rock formation. Our hotel for tonight has a theme. It's called L'Hôtel Détective."

"L'Hôtel Détective? Why's that?"

I filled him in. "In addition to its emblematic cliff, the town of Étretat is known for its association with the gentleman detective, Arsène Lupin. His character was created by the writer Maurice LeBlanc, who lived in town. He set his mystery stories about his fictional detective character here."

"So they have a hotel with a detective theme in Étretat? And we're staying there?"

"Exactly," I told him. "We're in the *Murder on the Orient Express* room. It was the last one available for tonight."

"Well, that's a different idea for a hotel," Sam said. "I wonder what it will be like."

When we got to the Detective Hotel, we found that our room was on the top floor. The *Orient Express* room was very small, like a train compartment. There was a luggage rack on the wall across from the bed, a bed which took up almost the whole room. Inside the old leather suitcase on the luggage rack, the management had cleverly hidden a TV, which was revealed when you pulled a cord that opened the suitcase.

We looked around the room for the bathroom. It wasn't far to look in such a compact space, but there was no bathroom to be found. We were mystified.

"I'm sure the room I reserved had a private bathroom," I said to Sam. "Let's call down to reception and ask." I reached for the period piece telephone on the little bed table.

"Just a minute, Barbara. This is too silly. Let me look around." Sam was studying the chart on the back of the door, which showed the floor layout and fire escape routes. "Maybe the bathroom is in the hall?" he postulated. "Wait a minute. What's this big mirror here?"

The mirror had an elaborate gold handle in the form of a cobra. He pulled on it, and *voilà*. The floor-length mirror was mounted on a door that opened to reveal the cute and well-appointed shower, toilet, and sink!

We had a good laugh about that as we descended the hotel's curving staircase to the lobby on our way to the beach to admire Étretat's famous cliff.

CHAPTER SEVENTEEN

ASKING THE N'KISI KONGO FIGURE FOR ANSWERS

S am and Barbara flew back to Florida for the winter as scheduled. Meanwhile, Alice and Abdoulaye had traveled from Le Havre to Paris, where they changed trains for their return to Caussade.

The *gare de Caussade* train station was a three-minute walk from *La Table d'Alice* restaurant. Alice's husband and little Manu were waiting on the *quai*, the station platform, as the train pulled in. Manu ran to his mother and hugged her around the legs.

She bent down to embrace him tenderly with one arm as she put her other arm around her husband. She lost no time introducing Abdoulaye to her little family. Everyone gave hugs of greeting and kisses on the cheek, *la bise*, to one another. Abdoulaye lifted his little half-nephew high into the air, and Manu laughed with pleasure at the special attention from this new 'big brother' figure.

Back at the restaurant, Abdoulaye waited for a quiet opportunity to fulfill his promise to Ekon Ibrahim. When the moment was right, he approached Édouard and placed the plasticized scrap of the Niger Delta geological survey into his waiting hands. He then breathed a sigh of relief. What an odyssey! He had done it. He thought of Ekon Ibrahim back in Niger and hoped he was well.

In the coming days, Édouard busily arranged for the big reveal: a ceremony that would unite the oil deposit map with the N'Kisi Kongo statue. He had proved himself the tribe's trusted confederate during his time working as an oil company engineer in Nigeria's River State on the Ogoni's tribal lands.

To reassure all the concerned parties, particularly the Ogoni tribesmen, that everything was being done in an above-the-board manner the Ogoni king and high court officials were invited to the ceremony at which the pattern of the statue's nail heads would be held against the map in the correct orientation. This action would show a nail indicating the precise coordinates on the seabed where the platform should be erected.

A date was selected, and notifications were sent out. Ogoni dignitaries from Nigeria were invited along with those officials living in exile or abroad closer by in France and England.

No sooner than the French invitations were received, a small, wizened, African man dressed in white presented himself at *La Table d'Alice*. In a fortunate twist of fate, it turned out that an Ogoni shaman with expertise in Ogoni tribal traditions and practices was living only 14 kilometers away from *La Table d'Alice* near the little town of Montpezat de Quercy.

The Ogoni medicinal healer and spiritual guide was now part of the household of the former British governor of Nigeria with whom he had campaigned all over West Africa until their joint retirement to sunny southwest France. With the advice of this traditional shaman, Édouard made the necessary arrangements to receive the Ogoni king and his courtiers correctly. To further ensure the privacy and sanctity of the proceedings, Édouard enlisted Hervé from the Caussade police force to guard the restaurant entrance against potential unwelcome intruders.

On the appointed afternoon, the distinguished invitees were shown into the main dining room at *La Table d'Alice*. Édouard had transformed it into an Ogoni royal reception room according to the Ogoni shaman's directions. At the far end of the space, a throne had been erected. The enormous armchair sat on a dais up four steps from the floor. The red velvet chair was decorated with leopard skins provided by the shaman.

The N'Kisi Kongo statuette was displayed on a pedestal table in front of the steps. It was the modern copy with the nails in the stomach. The whereabouts of the older statuette, which had been stolen from the restaurant exhibition, were still unknown.

Folding chairs were set in neat rows for the audience, leaving space for an aisle in the middle, like at a wedding. Abdoulaye, dressed in a traditional embroidered djellaba robe with a red, pillbox-shaped hat on his head, greeted the arriving dignitaries and showed people to their seats.

There was a group of about thirty attendees. Manu and his babysitter were there, of course. Manu was holding a little pet dog. The babysitter carried the dog's basket.

The Englishman who loved the composer Delius arrived and walked slowly to his place, supported by his French wife/companion on one side and by his cane on the other. He was introduced as Sir Hiram Pickett-Smythe, the former and final British Governor of Nigeria before independence.

Next came about 20 Africans, dressed in their traditional

garb: the men in colorful *kente* cloth, the women in Western-style silk dresses with matching turbans covering their hair.

When Abdoulaye, who was acting in the role of official page, announced the name, François Lamy, the dealer in African native arts, wearing his usual rumpled white suit, sidled down the aisle.

The crowd spoke together in hushed tones. The atmosphere was expectant.

After a short interval, the dry, insistent sound of bones or seeds rattling in a tube drew everyone's attention to the front of the room. A curtain arranged to the side of the stage parted, and the aged Ogoni shaman stepped forward and bowed to everyone. His simple white dress and loosely knitted white cap were dazzling against his very dark skin. He exuded a presence that was almost as mesmerizing as the glowering N'Kisi Kongo figure on the pedestal next to him.

Without further ado, he rang a bronze gong three times, and everyone fell silent.

Alice and Édouard proceeded down the center aisle and took their seats in the first row near the statuette. Abdoulaye followed after them, smiling prodigiously at everyone as he went along. He took a seat to the left of the statuette in the front row.

Next, the Ogoni shaman made the gong ring out with a thrumming sound, and everyone stood up at this signal. The attendees turned to look back toward the entrance door where Hervé, the gendarme, stood at attention.

A regal personnage with a banner across his chest and a black bowler hat on his head stood in the doorway, then slowly made his way down the center aisle, staring straight ahead.

The Ogoni king was a handsome man of about sixty years old, one who looked as if he enjoyed the pleasures of good living. As he swept by each row in his lavender robe, the guests bowed from the waist toward his passing figure. He wore a magnificent chain necklace of oblong-shaped, orange beads around his neck; in his right hand, he held a crocodile-headed scepter.

The room was silent as he ascended the steps to the dais and took his seat on the awaiting throne. When he had arranged himself comfortably, he rapped twice loudly with his staff, and everyone was seated.

The shaman in charge of the gong intoned in the Ogoni language and then in French and English:

"All hail King Emere Godwin Bebe Okpabi,
Chief of Ogoniland."

His voice rang out with pride and authority from his small frame, although it was clear that he was most comfortable when speaking Ogoni. The proceedings were very simple but impressive. We all sat gazing at His Highness, and he gazed back at us, relaxed and looking very at ease.

King Emere gave a sign to Édouard and Abdoulaye, and they stood up and approached the throne. Édouard put out his hand, and Abdoulaye drew the piece of geological survey out from the folds of his robe. He put it into Edouard's outstretched palm, reenacting for the assembled throng the scene that had played out between them several weeks ago. Abdoulaye was then seated, and Édouard held the piece of geological survey in front of the audience to show it to them. He then went up to the N'kisi Kongo and held the map up to the nails of the statuette while King Emere, the Ogoni shaman, and everyone else watched the proceedings intently.

The audience held its collective breath. Édouard fiddled

with the position of the map. The Ogoni shaman stepped in closer as if to assist. The two men conferred in low tones. Édouard once again adjusted the position of the piece of geological survey in front of the nails in the statuette's stomach. He frowned. The Ogoni medicine man grimaced. Up on his throne, King Emere lost his look of supreme confidence.

Climbing the steps onto the dais, the Frenchman whispered briefly into King Emere's ear. The king's eyes widened. He asked Édouard for confirmation of some kind. His eyes flashing, he shook his powerful fist and shouted something in the Ogoni tongue. The Ogonis in the audience gasped. Édouard translated the bad news into French.

"Ça ne marche pas. It's not working. The pattern of nails in the N'Kisi Kongo figure does not indicate the coordinates of the oil deposit as expected."

The crowd broke into an uproar. Everyone was talking at once. People threw their hands up in the air in exasperation. They shook their heads in disbelief. They stamped their feet in frustration. The happy atmosphere of the gathering turned angry and then downcast. Only one member of the audience looked satisfied by this turn of events. François Lamy sat with an ill-disguised smirk on his face.

The Ogoni shaman seemed unfazed by the brouhaha. Paying no attention to all the excitement, he retreated behind the curtain and returned shortly, holding the statuette of a two-headed dog before him. The wooden sculpture was studded with nailheads like the N'Kisi Kongo figure of the man with a raised fist. The little wooden dog was long, like a dachshund. Its body was painted a weathered gray in the spaces where it was not covered with nails and rusty metal pieces. The identical dog's heads on each end of the body had floppy black ears and open mouths with teeth showing in a sort of smile. The effect wasn't so much scary as appealing and friendly.

Making some sounds deep in his chest, the shaman bowed toward the king and then held the two-headed dog statuette up toward the heavens as if appealing to something.

He put the dog figure on the pedestal next to the first N'Kisi figure, both of the statues bristling with metal nails. Taking the padded mallet in his hand, he rang the metal gong until everyone settled down and got quiet. Once he had everyone's full attention, he gestured to Sir Hiram, whose orderly he had been in the British Army. His employer and former superior officer rose from his seat.

"I say," said Sir Hiram, a bit abashed, standing up somewhat unsteadily with the help of his cane. He continued in his clipped, upper-class British English, which he then translated into fluent but heavily accented French:

"I have been privileged to learn much about the traditional practices of the Ogoni people specifically, and Nigeria in general, from my former subaltern, the Ogoni shaman here before us. He has become a trusted friend as well as my manservant over the years of our living together in Africa and now in France. He wants me to explain to you that sometimes, the power of more than one N'Kisi Kongo figure is necessary to achieve the desired outcome of a divination ceremony like this one. In order to wake the spirit world and stimulate the occult forces to reveal their message, the power of the two-headed dog 'power figure' you now see on the pedestal may be needed in combination with the first N'Kisi Kongo statuette."

Both King Emere and the Ogoni medicine man nodded their heads vigorously in approval and appreciation of Sir Hiram's remarks.

Sir Hiram went on to elucidate for the benefit of those in the audience who were unfamiliar with such practices that the dog-shaped statuettes were prized by the tribe for their power to sniff out the truth and identify evil doers, just as dogs in real life seemed to have special abilities as guardians and protectors. Saying this, he sat down in his seat with a self-effacing little bow.

All eyes turned back to the two African sculptures on the pedestal. Without a word, the Ogoni shaman picked them both up and crashed them together as hard as he could. The objective was to wake the powerful forces contained in their forms and stir up the connection between the human relics and sacred roots inside them with the cosmos.

The medicine man then pantomimed to Édouard, who had been standing nearby looking on with everyone else, to try to match the map of the oil field to the nail heads of the raised fist statuette once again.

Fingers trembling a little at first, Édouard held it to the figure's stomach and adjusted it with care, comparing the map with the statue's nails. After double-checking, he turned to the king with a flourish, and this time, he announced triumphantly in a loud voice, "Ça y est, votre Altesse! There it is, Your Highness! There can be no doubt. The longest nail head of the N'Kisi statuette has now marked the coordinates of the oil deposit! The future rehabilitation of the Ogoni tribal lands and its people will soon be underway!"

The audience erupted in applause. A few people whistled, and some men clapped each other on the back. Manu's little terrier started barking with all the excitement and tore off after François Lamy, who was headed down the center aisle toward the exit. Growling threateningly and nipping at the antique dealer's pant leg, Manu's determined little pet wouldn't let go, no matter how hard Lamy tried to shake him off.

Suddenly, Sir Hiram Pickett-Smythe shouted out above the fray, "Arrest that man! I recognize him. He's wanted by the Drouot auction house in Paris! Don't let him get away!"

Hervé from the Caussade gendarmerie stepped forward to finish what Manu's little dog had started and prevented François Lamy from getting any further toward the door. As the policeman led the Africana dealer away for questioning, Lamy was shouting imprecations about the unfairness of it all as he went.

CHAPTER EIGHTEEN

ALL'S WELL THAT ENDS WELL?

TOUT EST BIEN QUI FINIT BIEN?

M any of the guests were mystified by what had just happened. There was a general hubbub as they questioned each other, trying to understand. Even those who had been following the story of the theft and attempted kidnapping at *La Table d'Alice* four months earlier did not necessarily make the connection between the oil discovery, Sir Hiram Pickett Smythe's accusation, and François Lamy's arrest.

Édouard deftly stepped into the breach. From his position at the front of the room, he commanded the attention of the group while he explained to the attentive listeners:

"Two N'kisi Kongo raised fist figures, the modern one with nails in the stomach area and the authentic tribal carving without any nails in that prohibited area, were both on exhibition during our African art exhibition here at the restaurant. The authentic N'kisi statue was loaned to the restaurant anonymously by Sir Hiram Pickett-Smythe. It was part of his personal collection of Africana assembled during his many years as Nigerian governor-general. We were honored to be able to display it in our show. We never dreamed that it would be in danger here in sleepy Caussade.

Alice and I also displayed our modern copy of a N'Kisi, the one whose stomach nailhead pattern had been arranged to match up with the oil map survey. This was probably unwise. We didn't count on François Lamy being on our trail and robbing us. Luckily, his henchmen filched the wrong statue for the oil discovery, but they stole a valuable antique in itself since the governor-general's statuette is highly prized by collectors."

People in the audience started to put two and two together. *Ah ha!*, they thought to themselves. Aloud, those in the know were happy to explain to others who were still confused.

The theft that took place at the restaurant was a case of mistaken identity. The thieves took the authentic N'kisi Kingo figure in the belief that its nailheads would reveal the oil deposit location. They were unaware that it was, in fact, the other statue, the modern rendition, which held the key to the oil coordinates.

The ringleader of the robbers, François Lamy, was now in *garde à vue*, under investigation at the police station. He had been on the trail of the oil discovery for some time, with help from a network of informants in both Nigeria and France. Tipped off by his spies in Africa, Lamy had also followed Abdoulaye to Normandy with the goal of taking the map from him. It had been his aim to get a hold of both the map and the statuette. The oil companies would have paid him dearly for information leading them to the oil discovery first.

Sir Hiram, whose pale face was still flushed with emotion, had been shocked to realize that he knew the man trying to sneak away early from the ceremony. Although years had elapsed since the Englishman had dealt with Francis Lannelongue at the famous Drouot auction house in Paris, the old man still recognized him in his new guise as François Lamy. By either name, he was a crooked dealer in African artwork who had cheated the governor-general and other collectors in the past. The Englishman told all those around him who would listen that the Africana dealer was wanted by Interpol on two continents for theft and forgery under his real name of Francis Lannelongue.

Fortunately, the criminal and the nefarious forces who had been trying to steal the oil had now been neutralized thanks to Manu's little dog, Hervé's presence as guard, and the governor-general's quick-thinking identification. Their attempt to gain control of the oil map had failed.

The attendees broke out into a smattering of applause. Everybody was talking at once in their various languages. What an exciting event!

Édouard invited King Emere and his ministers to come outside onto the patio. The king's suite of attendants and the others followed in his wake to a long table that had been set up near the pool under vine-covered trellises. The white napery glistened in the dappled sunshine of the lovely day and sparkled on the place settings of china, silverware, and crystal glasses.

Once everyone had located their place cards and taken their seats, the king, at the head of the table, rose and welcomed everyone to this great occasion, which presaged a happier future for his people. The overhanging vines brushed lightly against his bowler hat as the tall man bobbed up and down with happiness.

His Highness then introduced his prime minister, who stood up and thanked all those who had helped to make this fortuitous outcome possible, saying, "I do not wish to diminish the joy of this occasion in the slightest, but I want to stress how much this latest oil field discovery will mean in the Delta where our people have long been caught in a nightmarish dilemma. In the name of the Ogoni people and in memory of those like Ken Saro-Wiwa and the other martyrs who lost their lives in the struggle for justice and fair treatment of the Ogoni, let us raise our glasses and toast to the glorious new future on the horizon for Ogoniland."

"Here, here, *ainsi soit-Il*, Amen, *Insha Allah!*" the guests repeated as they raised their glasses of champagne or fruit juice for the observant Muslims among them. Everyone took a sip of their cocktails and wished one another *bon appétit.*

And a good appetite was needed to enjoy the feast that followed. Dish after delicious dish was brought out from the kitchen. The champagne, wine, and fruit juice flowed freely. The glasses jingled as participants called for another toast, singling out different people for special recognition.

The company got gayer and more boisterous as the courses went by. They started with an unusual *amuse bouche* of *mousse* of zucchini and sun-dried tomato *purée* sprinkled with dried seaweed and pine nuts. This was followed by an entrée of cold melon soup accompanied by *crème fraîche* flavored delicately with mint.

For the main course, Abdoulaye had prepared his fragrant, spiced chicken dish, *poulet sénégalais,* which was so highly appreciated that several diners suggested that he might eventually have a future as owner of franchise chicken restaurants.

People joked around, trying to come up with the catchiest name for his future business venture. The name 'Fab Ab,' short for 'Fabulous Abdoulaye,' was proposed. Or, playing on the long 'ay' sound at the end of 'poulet,' pronounced 'pou-lay' in French, 'Ab-poulet à l' Abdoulaye' or simply 'Ab-Pou-Laye' were some of the ideas. The young man enjoyed all the positive attention enormously. Who knew? Maybe he could become an entrepreneur? Anything was possible with hard work once he got his EU citizenship.

As the feast went on, the guests became more and more comfortable with each other and made friends around the table.

Little Manu was allowed to inspect the King's crocodile-headed scepter under the watchful eye of his *nounou*. The king was very patient with him. Then, the little boy was reluctantly led away for a nap after giving kisses to his *maman et papa*.

Sir Hiram's French wife and some of the other ladies wanted to know about the beautiful dashiki dress that Alice was wearing. She had given it her signature high-fashion twist thanks to her accessories. Alice explained that it was a new design by Imane Ayissi from Cameroun, a Paris-based designer whose high-voltage creations were sometimes worn by the likes of Zendaya and Angela Bassett.

Sir Hiram and some of the older Ogoni courtiers were involved in a spirited discussion comparing Nigerian World Cup soccer players and old-time English cricketers.

At the head of the table, Édouard and King Emere were speculating about the rosy future to come in the Niger Delta when the oil revenues started to roll in. They agreed that the Ogoni government would need to be greatly expanded to administer and oversee the funds generated by the oil wells in the most intelligent and fair way. There were so many details to discuss.

Then Édouard excused himself to marshall the kitchen staff to present the *pièce de résistance*, the dessert. From the kitchen, the servers wheeled out a small, cloth-covered table. It was topped by a beautiful pastry creation covered in *fondant*, white icing, decorated with slivered, toasted almonds. The crowd oohed and aahed appreciatively at its appearance.

On top of the cake, the pastry chef, *le pâtissier,* had constructed a model oil rig out of dark chocolate. Édouard lit a candle and placed the flame momentarily at the tip of the oil rig, setting off a sparkler that shot silver bolts up into the air in imitation of a gusher of oil.

The rocket was removed, and the cake slices were passed out around the table. The fluffy layers of *pâte génoise* were baked with a slightly crunchy toffee and nut mixture, which complimented the sweet taste of the *glaçage* to perfection. Coffee and miniature pastries were served around the table: *petits fours,* tiny *éclairs,* and chocolate squares topped with little pieces of gold leaf.

The afternoon slipped into evening. One by one and in small groups, people started to take their leave of the party. Alice and Édouard stood by the gate of the restaurant, saying goodbye to the departing guests and acknowledging their thanks for the beautiful and delicious banquet.

King Emere's long limousine swept him off through the narrow streets in front of the restaurant, and the party officially broke up. The few remaining participants made their way back home or to their various accommodations.

While his half-sister and her husband retired to rest, Abdoulaye, who had changed back into jeans and a tee shirt, donned an apron over his clothes and helped with the cleanup. The staff pitched in to ready *La Table d'Alice* to open for lunch, as usual, the following day.

The End

EPILOGUE

When François Lamy, whom Sir Hiram Pickett-Smythe knew as Francis Lannelongue, a notorious forger and thief of African *objets d'art,* agreed to return to him the N'Kisi Kongo statuette his accomplices had stolen from *La Table d'Alice* several months earlier, the ex-Nigerian governor did not file charges against him.

The valuable and venerable, authentic N'Kisi Kongo statue would be returned to Sir Hiram, who would, in his turn, repatriate it to Africa, where it would have pride of place in the new Museum of African Art being built in Kinshasa.

Lannelongue, aka Lamy, was turned over to the national authorities and Interpol to face a long list of charges for counterfeiting and smuggling in addition to possession of stolen goods.

After the reveal ceremony, Édouard entrusted the plasticized map to the Ogoni Prime Minister. He removed the nailheads from the modern statuette, but he couldn't throw the carving away. He put it on his office bookshelf as a talisman.

The former oil executive-turned-restaurateur and the

Ogoni leaders went right to work conferring with engineers and hiring experts in petroleum science to exploit the Ogoni oil discovery safely and profitably.

Unfortunately for the tribe, after a promising beginning, the oil wealth did not improve their lives as planned. The lure of such huge amounts of money as were involved was too much temptation for many Ogoni politicians and businessmen to resist. Corruption and backroom deals siphoned off profits.

King Emere was overthrown in a palace coup, and a more compliant royal was installed in his place. To gain lucrative contracts, influence peddlers looked to the highest bidder. Votes were bought. Arms were twisted by bribes of cash payoffs or job promises. The business-as-usual realities of the entrenched Nigerian power structure took over, and the average Ogoni tribesman's lot was not significantly changed for the better.

The waters of Ogoniland remained polluted with oil runoff chemicals. There was no safe drinking water, and those who could afford it relied on bottled water. The others had no choice but to drink the contaminated water. Many Ogoni fell sick by succumbing to the diseases caused by the pollution. The high incidence of cancers and other ailments created a medical crisis in the River State region.

Furthermore, since their lands and waters were unfit for agriculture or fishing after fifty years of oil company spoliation, few tribesmen had a way to earn an income. In order to survive, they used the resources that they did possess. They extracted and refined kerosene from wildcat oil deposits. Kerosene for cooking was needed by everyone, and it was easy to sell on the black market. This dangerous work enabled many to eke out a living.

Back in Sarasota, where Sam and Barbara were spending the winter months, they learned about this by watching YouTube programs about Ogoniland. They recommended the shows to their friends and acquaintances in an effort to raise people's awareness about energy dependence and its impact on a small tribe living far away in the Niger River Delta in Africa.

They also became better informed about the growing movement to repatriate artwork removed from its country of origin during the European powers' colonial conquests. From the sculptures of Angkor Wat in Cambodia to Indian and Indonesian temples, from the Elgin Marbles of the Parthenon in Greece to the palace of the *Obas* in Benin with its bronzes, precious artifacts spirited away to European and American museums were being reclaimed. The issue was complicated by questions of legal ownership and the availability of preservation techniques in Africa and Asia.

Sam and Barbara read that French President Macron suggested that *objets d'art* like the N'Kisi Kongo statuette could perhaps be shared in a joint ownership agreement of some kind. A Bénin bronze, for example, which had important religious and cultural importance to the people who had created it, could be displayed in Africa but on a loan from France.

It seemed that the time when a people's artistic heritage could be locked up in an institution a continent away from its source of inspiration was probably ending. Sam and Barbara hoped that when such issues were resolved, the treasures would be displayed and preserved for the enjoyment and benefit of all.

BOOK CLUB NOTES

1. How would you compare Sam and Barbara's summer trip in France to Abdoulaye's journey?
2. Describe N'Kisi Kongo statues and their function in the village where they came from.
3. Why is there special interest in African cultures in France?
4. What nationality are Melillans and where is Melilla?
5. How do oil revenues both help and hurt African states like Senegal, Niger, Nigeria and many others?
6. What happened to the migrant camps around Calais on the French side of the English Channel? Why? Where have the migrants gone?
7. How do you envision Abdoulaye's future in France?
8. Do you see any similarities between a pilgrimage to le Mont Saint Michel and faith in the power of N'Kisi Kongo figures?
9. What might be a solution to the migrant crisis?

ACKNOWLEDGMENTS

The author would like to thank her writing coach, Lisa Pulitzer, for her encouragement and support.

The members of the writing group she met through Long Island University helped to keep her moving along on this project.

She is also grateful to first readers, Nadine Helstroffer, her neighbor and friend, and Susan King, her friend and travel companion (China and French Polynesia) from Florida.

Todd Bain at the Hunter Public Library in Hunter, New York, was helpful in finding and renewing reference material.

Most of all, she would like to recognize the invaluable contribution of her partner, Nathan Kujawski, whose belief in her never wavered and without whose patient help this book would not have been possible.

Heartfelt thanks are also due to all her friends and acquaintances in the village of Montpezat de Quercy, France. The wonderful times she has spent there were part of the inspiration for this book.

ABOUT THE AUTHOR

Roberta Samuels earned degrees in French and Art History from Northwestern University and the University of Paris at the Sorbonne. *Vanished!,* her book series, evolved from her passion for French culture, beautiful objets d' art, and exotic travel. The starting point for the books is based on her experience living in  a medieval house in a French village interwoven with historical background and actual events and people. She worked as a French teacher, translator, tour escort and art gallery owner, showing her own artwork among others. She speaks French fluently. She lives in New York City and Montpezat de Quercy, France, with her partner.

 instagram.com/Rosamu ɪ _